EIGHT SHORT STORIES

KENSINGTON • SAN FRANCISCO JOURNAL •

THE CONSISTORY • A TAPE FOR BRONKO •

I AM RISEN • BURIED TREASURE • THE

FUNERAL • CANTOS XV (AS YOU LIKE IT!)

Anne Paolucci

With an Introduction by
HARRY T. MOORE

ACKNOWLEDGEMENTS

The author wishes to thank *The American P.E.N.* for permission to reproduce "Kensington" (which first appeared in the Summer 1974 issue of that magazine), and *The South Carolina Review* for permission to reproduce "The Consistory" (first published in the *Review*, December 1972).

Library of Congress Catalog Card Number: 76-53274
ISBN: 0-918680-04-2

P S
3 5 6 6
. A 5 9 5
E 3 8

To My Half-Baked Ghosts

ORIGINAL TYPE STYLE AND DESIGN BY SILVETT

A Griffon House Publication
H. Prim Co., Inc.
38 West Main St. • Bergenfield, N.J. 07621

CONTENTS

INTRODUCTION

It is good to have Anne Paolucci's remarkable stories (two of which have appeared in journals) brought together in the present collection. Most of us who know them will certainly want to read them again, and more than once. All of them are magnetic and delightful.

The author's fine sense of the dramatic enhances their effectiveness. She has written several plays, successfully staged in America and Italy, and her experience with them has certainly influenced the expert use of dialogue in her fiction, helping to make her vital characters in so many cases so importantly self-revealing in their skillfully motivated atmosphere.

There is tension in these stories, as well as comedy. One of those written most recently, "A Tape for Bronko," is largely a character sketch, as we would say, but a significant one in which the narrator presents Yugoslavia not in terms of its coasts and farmlands and mountains, but rather through the portrait of Bronko, the "monumental" driver who had been officially provided to transport the narrator around Belgrade. Bronko isn't his correct name (which sounds something like it), and part of the fun comes through that little example of parapraxia. Bronko is massively "real" from the very beginning and continues to exert an influence, a wryly comic Balkan influence, on the story even after he disappears from it. His easy skill at the wheel of a car contrasts with the awkward irresponsibility of another driver whom a guide refers to as a "professional," a neat bit of irony.

Again and again in these stories, the characters are impressively vital. This might also be said of a quite different kind of story from that of "Bronko," also a sketch and of virtually the same length: "Buried Treasure." Here the narrator describes her father-in-law, an ancient Italian from a village near Naples who, after his retirement, takes up painting. He is a forceful, single-minded figure, genially presented, and when he finally gives up his house in Yonkers to move into an apartment in Queens, he buries in the back yard what is most beloved to him—and this leads the author to another story, also about "buried treasures," that gives the tale what we know as a surprise ending, deftly done.

"Kensington" is quite different; a small drama acted out mostly in a London pub, with a few bedroom scenes in the area.

The people in the story, an Englishman and an English girl and the American through whose consciousness the action is projected, are neatly differentiated. There is some straightforward description-narration, even a bit of stream of consciousness and the muddle of a dream, but the conversation dominates and, as usual in Anne Paolucci's fiction, it is skillfully functional. The two British characters come through strongly, even though the girl appears only briefly, and Stephen is fully characterized in his actions, speech, and thought—the ex-seminarian-become-professor, whom a friend in youth had tried to direct toward the priesthood. Four years after he has first known Dave and Kitty, he is in London and, without knowing quite why, he goes to that pub in Kensington, and the comedy-drama, flashbacks and all, begins, tangled in sex complications.

A story in quite another kind of setting—"The Consistory"—is equally complicated, but in other ways, and again the conversation-dramatization carries the tale, this time a tense one that turns smoothly into fantasy. In "The Funeral" (but is it a funeral?) a group of men and women, all highly individualized as they speak their thoughts, ride to the cemetery in a car bristling with antagonisms. The author's versatility in "San Francisco Journal," divided into two parts—one, literary-philosophical-religious; the other, largely women's sex life—is revealed in the framework of a story of two girls sharing an apartment, a story that is not only reflections but also confrontations and full of the sharp dialogue characteristic of Anne Paolucci's writing.

"Canto XV (As You Like It)" combines in its title Shakespeare and Dante; but the caption provides an altogether new dimension. In it, Dante addresses Brunetto Latino in the seventh circle of the Inferno—"O Ser Brunetto, are you here?" He is indeed, in a story whose tense dialogue all occurs over the telephone except for two lines near the end that are an ironic conclusion whose outcome has to be guessed, though it is not difficult to imagine exactly what it will be. Similarly, "I am Risen"—note again the revealing title—has an ending with a prod to the imagination, in a story that begins with an anecdote which is really a parable, in a tale with undercurrents of reference to Freud, the Bible, and Yeats, but, above all, a further demonstration of Anne Paolucci's ability to reach deeply into the human situation.

I have tried to avoid "giving the stories away," have merely indicated for the reader some points of interest; and indeed they are points of high interest. This particular author has a definite gift for the short story, rather closely related to her experience in the drama, an engaging versatility, a fine sense of character, for what makes people live and behave in certain ways, as well as an economic skill in never giving too much. The questing reader will certainly find these stories, once again, magnetic and delightful!

HARRY T. MOORE
Southern Illinois University

THE CONSISTORY

"The Bishop is here, Father--"
"Show him in...."
Was it milk now or was it cream? Mrs.
Bloomgartner set the tea tray by the window.
TWO pitchers, damn her! She knew he never
remembered such things, and still she--
"How are you, Richard?"
"Your Excellency!" He knelt to kiss
the outstretched hand. The cold ruby burned
his lips. He pulled away and continued to
stare at the ring. Cream. He was almost
positive. But...suppose it was milk?
"I hear you've been working hard on
the project--" The Bishop sat down with a
flourish of his gown, sweeping the side forward.
"Yes...."
"Well, now, that's good news." He
leaned forward slightly. "But I hope you
have been taking care of your health. Last
time, you remember--"
"Oh, no. Nothing like that!" His
mouth twitched into what he hoped was a kind
of smile. "I've never derived so much
satisfaction out of anything--" A strange
expression came into the Bishop's eyes.
"Oh, nothing like that!" he added quickly,
crossing his hands tightly in his lap. "Not
like last time." God! If only he could say
straight out what he meant!
"Good. I was afraid my being away for
three weeks might--"
"I kept busy. So much to do!"
"Well, then! Tell me about it! You
promised to keep me informed, remember?
Three weeks is a long time--" he added, in
answer to his frustration.
He looked up. Mrs. Bloomgartner
hovered by the window, waiting to pour the
tea. The Bishop followed his gaze.
"Milk or cream, Excellency?"
"Black, please. Coffee should be
taken strong and unadulterated. As it was
meant to be enjoyed."
He swallowed in panic. What more
proof did he need, that fat bitch!. Why
hadn't she brought coffee in the first place?

3

He watched her move surreptitiously to the door and out of the room.

"Mrs. Bloomgartner will have coffee in a minute--"

The Bishop turned in his seat. "You needn't bother." He settled back in his seat. "Tea is fine."

"No, no. The tea is...for me." He hated tea. Though less the tea itself than the necessity of having it forced on him like this.

"You mustn't go to all this trouble when I drop in, Richard. Remember?"

"But it's no trouble at all, Your Excellency. Only, I HAVE been meaning to speak to you about...." He held up his hands as if to ward off the obvious con-clusion. "I'm not complaining, you under-stand. She's efficient enough--" Damn her! "But she does get in the way...and more than once I have found her--"

The Bishop raised his eyebrows and glanced toward the door. "You promised--"

"Yes, yes, yes. But you must listen. Before she comes back."

"You won't get all excited...like last time--?"

Nothing like that! Today was a new beginning. He had thought it all out very carefully. Vita nuova. He wiped his palms on his cassock, as though rubbing his legs. Were those really his legs? They felt so thin thin thin. The Bishop was touching his arm.

"Is something wrong?" He felt himself swaying and sat up very straight.

"No, no." But it always began with lies. With his trying to cover up. He tried to remember the last visit, three weeks before. But...the Bishop had had tea then! Was he trying to confuse him?

Mrs. Bloomgartner returned with a second tray. He felt a wave of hatred red-dening his face. The Bishop looked away.

"That's fine,.Mrs. Bloomgartner," he said very slowly, taking the proffered cup and handing it to the Bishop. He must stop

4

her before she poured for HIM, or she would
certainly give him away. "I'll have lemon,
instead of cream," he said distinctly. Was
there a trace of a smile on her lips? The
Bishop was savoring the coffee, his eyes
half closed. Mrs. Bloomgartner handed him
the tea.

"Ah, pine cookies. My favorite."
The Bishop reached over to pick up a cookie
from a silver tray. She HAD remembered
something.

"That will be all, Mrs. Bloomgartner,"
he said firmly. She seemed surprised, but
when the Bishop looked up and smiled, she
turned abruptly and left. "Thank you," he
remembered to call after her. But the door
had already closed. He set down the cup.
"It's quite impossible, you see." He gripped
the sides of the chair, determined not to
lose control. The Bishop sipped his coffee.
"I know I promised not to bring it up again.
Not without being absolutely sure. Now I
am. I have...proof!" There. He had taken
the plunge. In medias res. No more lies.
Already he felt better.

"Proof?" The Bishop studied the
silver tray for several seconds before he
scooped up a handful of loose pignoli from
the bottom. "You are absolutely sure?"

"Absolutely sure." He glanced uneasily at the door, then drew the heavy
chair closer to that of the Bishop. "You see,
she's Jewish."

The Bishop studied the pignoli in the
palm of his hand.

"WAS. We've been all through that,
Richard. She WAS Jewish. But you yourself
have given her communion. She is with us in
the body of Christ." He picked up one of
the nuts and transferred it slowly to his
mouth.

"That's precisely what she wants us
to think! Oh, yes! She takes communion!
She eats the wafer, so what? If you don't
believe it's the body of Christ, why you can
wipe your ass with it for all it's worth!"
The Bishop sighed, put the rest of

5

the nuts into his mouth, then wiped his hands
on a clean handkerchief which he refolded
neatly and put into a hidden pocket on the
side of his cassock. "Richard, nothing you
have said can be construed as proof. So far,
you are merely indulging in the same un-
founded--"
     "I've caught her at it...going through
my report!" He sat back flushed with excitement. "Spying on me when she thought I
wasn't looking. I've seen her going through
my letters, my...my wallet even." The
Bishop nodded gravely. "I let her do it,
thinking it best not to arouse her suspicions.
You should have come sooner--"
     "I came to you, first. I haven't
even unpacked yet."
     "It's urgent, you see. If my report
gets into enemy hands--"
     "Enemy hands?" There, he'd said it.
     "She's Jewish."
     "No, Richard. She is no longer
Jewish." The Bishop reached out as if to
touch him, but changed his mind. He moved
back slightly. "And even if she were, it
wouldn't make her the enemy. The Jews are
not our enemy."
     Again he reached out, this time
touching his arm. "How can YOU, of all
people, be so unkind? Don't you realize
where this can lead?" Was HE with them?
Had he been wrong about the Bishop too?
"...and does so much for you. She is wholly
dedicated to you."
     "Exactly!" The words took their own
course, careless of his intention. "Just
what they want her to do! Don't you see?"
The Bishop scooped up the remaining pignoli
at the bottom of the tray.
     "All right." He crossed his legs.
"What could Mrs. Bloomgartner possibly want
with your report?" Under the red robe,
Richard spotted thick white socks. Had the
Bishop been playing tennis? The question
became obsessive. White socks. Why white
socks? "And you will agree that I have
cooperated with you in every way," he was

6

saying. The Bishop uncrossed his legs and
picked up his cup again. "You don't doubt
my interest in all this, do you? Because if
there is any doubt in your mind--"
    "Oh, no!" Was he lying? He must
avoid lying.
    "You've had access to the library, to
the microfilm collection, to the rare book
room...we even requested books for you on
interlibrary loan...why we even wrote to the
Vatican for photostats of--"
    "And I'm grateful!"
    "Well then!"
    "Bloomgartner."
    The Bishop put down his cup. "All
right. Get on with it." He closed his eyes
and leaned back in his chair. "I'm listening."
    "She's a spy."
    "So you tell me."
    "I have proof."
    "You did say something about that."
    "You sound...skeptical."
    "No, Richard." The Bishop smiled half-
heartedly and opened his eyes. "Shall I be
the devil's advocate for a minute?"
    "I DO have it, you know--"
    "Yes, now that's important. What
exactly do you have?"
    "I told you. I practically caught her
at it. Going through everything."
    "In court, Richard, in court...that
would not be admitted as PROOF. You know
that."
    "We must do something!"
    "Very well. Since you feel this strongly
about it--"
    "It's not what I FEEL, Your Excellency.
I must insist on that point!"
    "Of course. I only meant--"
    "It's FACTS."
    "I was about to say, all things con-
sidered, it might be wise to replace her--"
    It was as though the ocean had come
crashing through the window. For a moment
he couldn't see anything at all. The pounding
in his head was a noise and a pain and a
blackness.

"That's not what I meant....That's not
what I meant at all--"
The Bishop spread out his hands in a
helpless gesture. "What else can we do?"
"Not that. Not that." Through a red
mist he saw the Bishop watching him. "It
would give everything away. And it would
expose others. She's very subtle. No, no.
She mustn't know that we suspect her!"
"Ah, so we DO agree--" The Bishop
patted his arm.
Did they?
"We'll watch her, naturally, and when
the proper moment comes--and you WILL let me
be the best judge of that, won't you, Richard?
--when the right moment comes, we'll take
action--have her transferred. Or whatever
seems best." He frowned. "You do trust me,
don't you?"
Did he?
"In the end, of course, such decisions
must rest with me. But I would want you to
go along willingly. You must have confidence
in my judgment--"
Would he?
The Bishop rose and crossed over to
the window, a dark blot against the Irish lace
curtains. He stood staring out for a minute,
then turned, his hands behind his back. "I
was hoping, Richard--to be perfectly truth-
ful--I had hoped you would have your report
ready for me today. It's been almost five
months now. And, although I HAVE neglected
you--oh, not intentionally, but I HAVE been
away for almost a month--you have had ample
time to work." He stroked his chin. "I may
be able to expedite things for you once the
report is in my hands." His head was a black
sphere against the gray afternoon outside.
Dark wings seemed suddenly to sprout from the
top of his shoulders and gently gently his
whole body rose and fell with some mysterious
cadence. "...better for all of us." It was
only the sound of the Bishop's voice. Only
the lace curtains moved. "A word from me now
can open up all sorts of doors for you. Are
you listening to me, Richard?"

8

The uneasiness inside him suddenly
curled up into a knot of fear. "Yes, Your
Excellency." He added quickly: "Whatever you
say."

"You will give me the report then?"
He came back to his chair and sat down. It
was ready. He could see the edges of it under
the tray, under the newspapers, where he had
put it just before the Bishop's arrival. But
....What?

"...must let her have free access to
everything. As though nothing had happened.
That way she will incriminate herself, you
see."

"It makes sense, yes."

"Meanwhile the report will be safe
with me."

Mrs. Bloomgartner was at the door.
Why hadn't she knocked? She stood aside,
glancing back over her shoulder.

"The Holy Father is here, Excellency."
The Bishop rose.

"I wanted to surprise you, Richard."
He helped him out of the chair.

"You ARE pleased I hope?" He fought
back his frustration. The timing was so
wrong. Everything. A large gray-haired man
was approaching them. Mrs. Bloomgartner had
retreated, closing the door behind her.

Was it really shut tight? He fought
an almost irrepressible urge to try it.
Instead, he fell on his knees in front of the
newcomer, who was robed in a long white coat
and wore a silver beaded yamulka. He looked
like Yul Brunner.

"Father, I--" He clutched the outstretched hand. "...never expected...."

The newcomer helped him to his feet.

"I've been meaning to stop by." He
turned away. "Is there some coffee left?"

The Bishop looked toward the door,
hesitating. "No, don't bother calling the
woman. I'll pour it myself."

"No, no. Let me."

"Thank you, Richard." Dear God, what
would he put in it? The Holy Father rescued
him. "Not too much cream. And one sugar."

"Try the cookies. They're home made.
Richard's aunt sent them."
The Holy Father took the cup from
Richard and glanced down at the tray of
cookies, uncertainly. "You've picked all the
nuts off, as usual--"
The Bishop looked embarrassed. "There's
still...." His voice trailed off.
The Holy Father laughed. "We're all
sinners...."
"Except the saints--"
"Even the saints, Richard, before
their sainthood."
"And Luther. Was he a sinner?"
"He said he was." The Holy Father
laughed again. "Why should WE doubt it?"
"Ah, but was he really?"
"The greatest sinner of all. He
sinned in thinking he did not sin."
"And Mrs. Bloomgartner?"
They exchanged glances.
"What about Mrs. Bloomgartner?"
If only St. Augustine were here. He
always had the right answers. He knew just
how to cope with the hierarchy. The red
tape. The formalities. Protocol. All
that nonsense. The white robes and the
red. The red and the black. He would cut
across budgets and official memos to the
heartbeat, the reality buried under the
masks of authority.
The Holy Father came up close. "Now,
what's all this? Morris tells me--"
The Bishop, just behind him, cleared
his throat.
"Richard has finished the report."
Who was Morris?
The Holy Father put down his cup and
fingered the heavy chain around his neck.
Something was wrong. He was good at sensing
shifting moods, atmosphere, emotional tension.
"She's Jewish, you see," he said
weakly, punctuating the unexpressed argument.
The Bishop moved nervously across the room
and stood for a few seconds by the door.
"Richard thinks Mrs. Bloomgartner bears

watching. He saw her going through his reports."

"Ah."

"She's a Jewish spy."

"I told Richard," said the Bishop, moving away from the door, "that the best thing to do was to carry on as though we didn't suspect. For a few more days at least." The Holy Father nodded approval.

"It is possible, of course. A spy among us. Still, the odds are so very much against it...."

Something was definitely wrong.

"...substantial evidence. We musn't give anything away until we have it. Am I right, Father?"

It was impossible! But why was he sweating like this?

"--out of reach...."

But they were part of it too!

"--safe in our hands."

"Yes, Richard. You must let us have the report. We can't run the risk now of letting her get it."

Yes, it was all painfully clear. They couldn't make out the report from Mrs. Bloomgartner's appraisal of it, so they would now work on him. But he KNEW. He would be careful.

"There's very little there, I'm afraid."

"But you said you had finished it."

"Ah, but it's in code."

"We can have it transcribed. Just give us the code."

"No, no. I must do that for myself. You see, I change the code every three days. It's all here." He pointed to his head.

"May we see the report?"

Well, why not. They couldn't possibly decode it.

"Excuse me." He moved the tray slightly to one side and picked up the sheets that he had placed there earlier in the afternoon. The Bishop reached out and took them. He examined first one side then the other, going through the same routine for each of the seventeen sheets of paper in his hands. Then he handed the sheaf to the Holy Father.

There was a curious expression on his face.
"Are you sure you will remember the
code this time?"
"Oh, yes." He smiled happily. Well,
relieved at least.
"But--" The Bishop put a hand on the
Holy Father's arm.
"You needn't be tactful. I know what
it must seem like to you. Blank sheets.
Right?" The Bishop nodded. The Holy Father
looked up puzzled. "Do you want a secretary
to help you?"
No. "That's very kind of you...."
He thought quickly. Well, why not? It would
certainly make it difficult for Mrs. Bloomgartner to carry on. That in itself was a
kind of victory. "Yes, I would appreciate
that." The telephone rang. The Holy Father
picked up the receiver. "Yes?" His voice
suddenly turned cold and harsh. "Damn you,
Hartley," he said in a hoarse whisper.
"What did I tell you about calls?" He lowered
his voice even more. "Well, get Dr. Ainsley!
I'm not the only saint on duty!" He glanced
over his shoulder and then away. "No,
there's no need. Everything's under control.
And I hope it's the same there! And Hartley.
It's All Saints Day. So stay off the stuff.
Why...you son of a bitch!" He hung up with
a bang and stood leaning against the desk
for a few seconds. "I'm sorry," he said,
turning back to them with a smile. "The
Chancery is always tracking me down. One
has to be firm. Where were we. Oh yes.
Someone to help you prepare the report."
"I'll need more books too."
The Bishop picked up a pad of paper
and a pencil from the desk. "Shoot."
"An Armenian Bible. An Arabic dictio-
nary. If possible, Jerome's commentary on
the Psalms. And Paul. Paul Goodman. And
Lady Chatterly's Lover. There are some interesting parallels between--" He stopped
short. Why should he give them even the
slightest lead?
"Is that all?"
"For now, yes." His head hurt terribly

and he stroked it gently, starting from the
nape of his neck upward toward the top, in
slow circular strokes. He reached the top
of his head, where the hair had been shaven
off when he had taken on the monk's garb.
"Oh, one more thing."
"Do you want some aspirin?"
He almost laughed. "No. But my hair
has grown in. I really need a barber,
wouldn't you say?"
"I'll see to it." The light had
grown dim and he could scarcely make out
the features of his guests. "We want to help
in every way, Richard."
It was almost over. Soon they would
leave.
"But you must not give in to those
horrid imaginings. Just remember that Mrs.
Bloomgartner is going to be under constant
surveillance. You can rest easy about everything. The important thing is not to give
in to frustration. We all have fears....The
point is to deal with them efficiently.
Without destroying the good things we build
each new day. Now take Mrs. Bloomgartner--"
"NO!!" Was he shouting? The light
was dim and he couldn't tell. "I will NOT
have her!" He leaped from his chair and
looked desperately for escape. "She's
probably out there right now--" pointing to
the door-- "listening!" Were they Jewish
too? He could scarcely make out the contours
of their heads. A hard and rasping sound
reached him. It was his own voice. "Don't
you think I KNOW? Oh, yes, you're awfully
good at it, both of you. And HER!"
Mrs. Bloomgartner walked in, as though
drawn there by some terrible nemesis. The
Holy Father switched on the light. He looked
annoyed.
"I told you to wait outside!"
"I have as much right to be here as
you do!"
"Damn you, can't you see--"
What were they chattering about in a
huddle? His throat was dry and his eyes were
swimming in some murky well. If only they'd

13

leave!

The Bishop had joined the others near the door.

"I hope you know what you're doing," said Mrs. Bloomgartner, turning her head to him.

"It's my responsibility."

"We are all involved!"

There was a quick angry exchange, inaudible.

"--may succeed this time! And then what? What will you do with your responsibility then?"

"It MUST run its course."

"Bullshit!"

"I agree. I think we should take action right now."

What were they shouting about? Everything had been settled.

"Your Excellency...." They stopped and stared at him in surprise. The Bishop recovered first. He buttoned the top two buttons of his cassock, hiding the paisley tie from view. The Holy Father adjusted his robe and moved forward toward him.

"Yes, Richard. I'm sorry. We were having...a conference."

"About the secretary." He must get them out of his room.

"Of course, Richard. We agreed it was all right." The Bishop came to the desk and retrieved the pad and pencil on which he had written earlier.

"Who would you like me to send you? Thomas? John? Let's see. Who came last week?"

He made a show of considering the suggestions.

"I'd like Judas. Yes, send Judas." He smiled in the dim light. He could see Mrs. Bloomgartner staring at him. Was the light on? But maybe they had misunderstood. He had to make sure--

"Judas." The Bishop patted his shoulder. "Very well, You'll have him in the morning. Judas Iscariot."

So. He had won. They had not suspected

for a moment what he had in mind. That he
could destroy the whole project with one
thrust, break the careful pattern he had so
carefully worked out for months to keep them
guessing. He had. He had won.
"Wait." They turned near the door.
Maccabeus, not Iscariot. That was
the whole business in one word. Judas Maccabeus.
It was not his voice at all. It was
drums and thunder and jungle rain. The
oracle in the empty temple and the devils
inside him struggling to be free. And as the
long tunnel of light rushed through him, the
sound of his own betrayal pierced his eardrums.
For a split second he saw the Bishop and the
Holy Father transfigured. He passed Mrs.
Bloomgartner on the way down, and there was
love in her dark face.

BURIED TREASURE

My father-in-law was an artist in many
ways, including oil painting, which he took
up as a hobby after he retired at the age of
65. I have an Assisi, two Greek temples, and
a Columbia University by him. They're quirky
--the Assisi especially. Umbrian buildings
in a Neapolitan setting. He was from Naples,
and his racial memories were rooted in that
soil--although he had not been back to the
old country since the age of twelve. And
everything he painted (unless one stood by
him and suggested orange skies and purple
waters) was Neapolitan in color and absolutely grotesque (in an intriguing way) in
configuration: wispy trees, fantastic shrubs,
lush, lurid greens and rotting browns.
Buildings were in a class by themselves.
He was damn good at them. I was impressed
from the start, because the hardest thing to
paint is a building. What color is a shadow?
Where does it begin and end? How far does it
extend? In what direction? He was good at
such things. Read a great deal and did research even, when he wasn't sure about something.
        He painted forty canvases or more,
after they moved to Queens. I have four large
ones, my sisters-in-law have several each, my
brothers-in-law have a total of ten, and my
mother-in-law has about eight. Some he sent
to relatives in the old village near Naples.
One of them, a scene of the clustered houses
on the mountain, was copied from a snapshot
he found lying around in his closet-attic.
God knows what he remembered and felt after
sixty-odd years! The scene was like a musty
memory pulled out of a kaleidoscopic assortment deep inside the soul. The town, when I
finally saw it in recent years, was very
modern--new houses, some apartment buildings,
too. Nothing like the painting. But then,
he wasn't trying to paint realistically at
all (although he would have insisted other-
wise); he was indulging in remembrances of
things not quite past.
        The portraits had the same odd quality
of the landscapes--only more of it. He copied

faithfully George Washington, Mona Lisa, Galileo, Da Vinci, Greek nymphs around a surreal fountain, peasants huddled near a "trulli" hut. They all stared out at the world, with an intensity of concentration which was the old man himself, the very opposite of still life and portrait painting--where the artist loses himself in the object. The portraits are all reflections of the old man's Stoic restraint, not finished at all in a professional way, but fascinating. I've seen the same look in my father-in-law's eyes, as he listened to a discussion about politics or about philosophy.

He had talent to sell, I'm sure; even without training, he was pretty good. And watching him, as I often did when we visited them in the Queens apartment, I was always impressed. I learned what little I know about smearing paint on canvas and beaver board from him. It took the place of the piano ritual, in a way. (I'll get to that.) I would watch him for hours, in the large closet he had turned into a studio. It was intriguing. I loved it. At one point, I even began to venture suggestions. He never took it badly. Every time I said something (he would provoke comments in an indirect way) about a sky or background colors or the planes in a face, he would work them over again and wait for my reactions the next time around. It wasn't really important to me, but I knew he wanted to please. He would work out on squares the blow-ups from pictures he cut out from books and magazines. In the end, of course, everything turned out to be his own taste. His own geometric precision (to a fault) and his own fantasy, always.

I mention these things because the old man is the focal point of the story. He was a determined and self-sufficient person, respectful of others but keen and stubborn about his own insight into things. An avid reader, he could put his own professor-son to shame. He knew Machiavelli as no one in the academic world knows him. A realist, but always kind, he understood the message of

"realpolitik" and lived by it. That's not easy!
He died as he had lived: quickly,
quietly, efficiently. When the cancer inside
him became an immediate problem (he never
went to bed until the very end and took
medication only sporadically), he agreed to
enter the hospital for an operation. They
brought him in one evening; the next morning
the nurse came in to prepare him for surgery
and he rose, went to the bathroom, got back
into bed, and died. Just like that. There
aren't too many people who can get up, go to
the bathroom, return to bed on their own steam
and then decide to die. The nurse fussed over
him as he got back into bed. "How do you feel?"
she asked. "Tired," he said. And died.
When my sister-in-law arrived that morning,
she found the mattress rolled up. She thought
they had taken him into the operating room
early. When she learned what had happened,
well, you know. It's hard to believe. But
that's the kind of man he was. No fuss. He'd
made up his mind, stoically, not to linger.
I'm convinced of it. The will is powerful in
some people. Helen Dunbar once wrote that we
choose the moment of our death. Not suicide;
she meant we WILL what we become. I'm
certain my father-in-law gave up with the same
powerful will and purpose he displayed all
his life.
        In the old big house in Yonkers, he
used to sit in a corner of the living room
and listen to me play the piano. I made a
point of playing for him every Sunday afternoon, when we visited the family. It was an
old large piano, but he was very proud of it.
You see, he'd worked on pianos for years
and knew how to build one from scratch. He'd
learned on his own. During the depression,
when everyone else was laid off, he was kept
on because he could do all the jobs alone.
He could build the frame (he was a carpenter
by trade), but he could also string the
instrument and build the sounding board. That's
not easy. The sounding board is the most
important part of a good piano. His piano was
an old second-hand upright. He bought it from

a junk dealer for ten dollars. He was too
proud to ask for one where he worked. By the
time I arrived on the scene, it was doubly
old. It sounded like a player-piano (it had,
in fact, been one), but that didn't faze him.
He tuned it regularly with his own home-made
tuning fork and instruments. And I never told
him that it wasn't quite right. It made no
difference.

He was terribly sentimental about music.
To me, that was a special bond between us. I
could excuse anything because of it. He'd
built a banjo and a mandolin for his own amuse-
ment, and sometimes he would strum them. But
when I visited, he would simply take his chair
in the corner of the living room, waiting for
me to play. He never asked, but I knew. And
I would go through my favorites--Mozart,
Beethoven, once in a while some Chopin--
knowing they were also his favorites, and I
would sometimes throw in his personal pref-
erences: Thais, Neapolitan songs, and some
operatic arias. My concert would last about
two hours--before dinner--and he would just
sit quietly and listen, staring straight ahead,
his eyes somewhere deep inside him, struggling
with emotion. Once or twice I caught that
intense look; it was uncanny. After all, he
was a carpenter and an uneducated man. But,
like I said, I wouldn't trade him for any of
my professional colleagues.

There was a tacit understanding between
us. We never spoke about music. I knew that
he wanted to hear me play; and I never disap-
pointed him. It was a ritual of sorts.
(Later, painting took its place.) I simply
wanted to please him. And, although my own
piano is a 1929 Steinway made in Germany, I
know that he heard the same perfect sounds
in his imagination when I played on his
broken-down upright. I did.

The piano, especially, figures in this.
The old man had turned almost 70 when he
decided to sell the house in Yonkers and move
into an apartment in Queens. It took a lot
of doing on all our parts, to convince him
that he should move. Everybody was worried

for him by that time, because he still insisted
on doing all the heavy chores around the house
and the yard--refurbishing the roof in its en-
tirety, where once he almost fell on account
of a dizzy spell, trimming the trees that got
battered in the winter storms, replacing doors,
trimming hedges. So for two years we all worked
on him--subtly, of course, because he had a mind
of his own and didn't want to be pushed into
anything. Eventually, he came around. I guess
he knew in his heart that it couldn't last
forever. The vegetable garden required a great
deal of attention, the grape arbor and the
hedges had to be pruned, the lawn had to be
mowed, the ivy on the north side of the house
(which housed hundreds of birds) had to be cut
down when the starlings began to pose a threat
to the structure. He had help, of course.
His son-in-law and nephew lived in the upstairs
apartment, and they had their chores too. But
the heavy jobs especially were the old man's.
He was never satisfied with any one else's
work. In the years they lived in Yonkers, he
never called in a workman from the outside. He
was proud of his skills.

When they finally decided to move, the
piano became a real problem. There was no room
for it in the new place, so it had to be destroyed. You see, he wasn't going to call in
someone to cart it away, and no one was interested in buying it. Besides, I suspect that
he had a sentimental attachment to it. I'm
sure of it.

First, he took it apart and chopped
the wooden frame into pieces which he threw
out. That was simple enough. But the real
trouble was the innards. The metal strings
could not be taken apart. And it was a big
piano, understand. One day, after watching
him struggle with it, my sister-in-law the
witch took her mother aside and whispered:
"Keep him out of the house tomorrow. Find
something for him to do. Willie and Donald
will get rid of the piano. He's going to
rupture himself if he goes on like this."
The old lady managed with some pretext. Willie
and his son worked most of the day, but they

could to nothing with the piano. Finally, they
took it out into the yard. When the old man
returned, late in the afternoon, he surveyed
the scene but said nothing. The next morning
he got back to work. He had sized up the
situation and had reached a decision. He dug
a deep hole and buried it, between the garage
and the strawberry patch. Just like that.

Bozo is buried there somewhere too.
It's only natural. What does one do with a
17-year-old dog, who has been part of the
family all that time? Someday, someone is
going to get a big surprise!

And the rock. That's not treasure
exactly, but it's a good story. The house
had a two-car garage, but the driveway was
narrow. It was an old house and only one car
could drive up the narrow space into the
garage. The second car had to be maneuvered
into position around the sharp corner of the
house and into the second garage, which was
attached to the first. My brother-in-law
Willie, who always boasted of his talents,
was naturally given the second garage. He
took on the challenge, since he liked to brag.
It would have worked all right, too, except
for the fact that there was a huge rock in
his way. It couldn't be straddled, it was
too big. He managed, of course (he was a
good driver, I'll say that for him), but he'd
curse privately. In front of the old man he
never complained. There was a silent running
feud between them, because my father-in-law
was so damn good at so many things and so
critical of others that Willie didn't want to
scompari--as they say in Italian--lose face.
So he suffered the garage in silence in the
old man's presence, complaining only in the
privacy of his own apartment upstairs, with
his wife and son. Lucy would report everything to her mother--simply to alert the old
folks to the fact that Willie had to be handled
with care. He had lots of problems and a low
boiling point. Well, the old man knew this
and never referred to the garage. He kept out
of Willie's way as much as he could. Except
when things really had to get done. In his

opinion, Willie was a nuisance more than a help and always in the way. But he never expressed such feelings publicly. We'd get some of the flak in whispered conversations before and after dinner, when my mother-in-law would plead with us not to mention this or that in the old man's presence. Willie wasted a lot of time. Although, to do him justice, I must say that he tolerated the old man even when he resented him. In his own way, he was very fond of him. The old man stepped in only when he saw that a task was too much for the others. Or when he saw that it wasn't going right.

One day Willie said to his wife: "Lou, tell your mother to keep your father off my back tomorrow. I don't want him around. I'm getting rid of that damn rock in the back." This triggered long whispered conversations between the women. My mother-in-law, poor soul, was frantic. There was bound to be a confrontation if the two men were together, Willie trying to get rid of the rock, my father-in-law chafing from the sidelines. It was an old story. Willie was certain to blow his top if the old man said anything to him while he worked. Even if he stood there watching from the kitchen window it would create sparks.

It was hard, but the women succeeded in driving my father-in-law out of the house on some errand into Manhattan. Willie quickly got to work. He dug carefully around the huge rock and then tied a heavy rope to it. His car was already in position, for pulling the rock out of the ground. He spent all morning and part of the afternoon trying to get the rock to budge. No luck. Finally, my sister-in-law, who had been watching from the up-stairs window, called down to him.

"Come upstairs and eat something. You need a rest." Willie went into the house. He was still upstairs when the old man returned. My father-in-law took everything in and made his decision.

"Keep him upstairs," he told his wife. "I can handle it." My mother-in-law couldn't stop him. She ran upstairs and managed to take

Lucy aside and tell her what was going on.
My sister-in-law kept Willie occupied for
a while longer. Naturally, she didn't dare
tell him that the old man had taken over the
job. They could hear nothing, which made my
poor mother-in-law all the more apprehensive.
How was the old man going to get rid of that
rock? Willie was strong, and he'd been at it
all day. She was sure the old man would rupture himself. And the car was no good to him.
He didn't drive.

Willie finally went back downstairs.
The women hurried after him. My father-in-
law, his hands in his pockets (his favorite
posture), a devilish gleam in his eyes, stood
by the garage door.

The rock was gone. The ground was
covered over as though nothing had happened.

Willie just stood there staring.
Finally, he asked: "Where is it?"

"I buried it," said my father-in-law,
obviously relishing his triumph.

"Buried it??!!?" Willie took this in
slowly, obviously in a mild state of shock.
It was the only time he was genuinely surprised. Too surprised to be annoyed. "How
the hell did you manage THAT?"

"I just dug around it a bit more and
slipped it into the ground," said the old
man, smiling now. Everybody was tense. The
women hovered near by, waiting for all hell
to break loose. Willie was hard to deal with
on such occasions. He always felt the old
man was showing him up--and when this happened, especially in the presence of the
women, he became sullen and morose for days.
But this time was different. He couldn't
get over it.

"My God!" he said finally, "why didn't
I think of that?"

"You tried to pry it out," said the
old man simply. "I just pushed it back in."

Years later, Willie still told the
story. And always with a touch of awe. And
always he would end the story with, "God, why
didn't I think of it?"

I don't know for sure what else is

buried in that yard in Yonkers. I suspect
some other things found their way there.
Once, driving through Westchester, we
decided to take a detour to see the old place.
It looked pretty much the same: the peach
tree near the side door, where the old man
had thrown a pit one summer evening, the bird
bath which he had built and placed in the
center of the lawn, the hedges trim and neat
looking, even the vegetable patch was in
bloom. The house too looked pretty much the
same--the veranda with its eighteen windows,
which the old man had built the first year
they had moved in; the new roof which he had
put on the last year they spent there, the
driveway which he had finally enlarged. The
"Beware of the Dog" sign was gone and the
rose bushes weren't quite as full as they used
to be. And the flowers around the bird bath
had disappeared, as had also the tree which
the old man had pruned (with the women hovering underneath the giant ladder) rather than
have it torn down, after it had been damaged
in the 1946 hurricane. But the hand of the
master was gone.
        Some day, when a big construction firm
decides to build high-rise apartment houses
in that neighborhood, and the owners will sell
their homes at high profits, bulldozers will
come up with the buried treasure of my father-
in-law. I was reminded of all this recently,
when my sister-in-law the witch, who now lives
on Long Island, told the story of the woman
who refused to sell out to Macy's in Queens
some years ago when the store was buying up
the houses in the area to build the Rego Park
branch. "They offered her $20,000!" she said
dramatically. "In those days, that was real
money!" She narrowed her eyes. "More than
what she had paid for it. But she refused to
sell. Macy's upped the figure to $35,000.
Still, she refused. Finally, they offered
her--would you believe it?--$100,000! But
she would NOT sell. It's still there, in the
middle of things. You've seen it? Of course,
when the old woman dies and the children sell
the place--they've got their own homes--just

think!" She leaned forward for effect.
"They'll bring in the big bulldozers and start
digging. And then--" (here she opened her
eyes wide) "they'll discover the skeleton buried
there!" Having made her point, she sat back
in her rocking chair, her hands folded over
her plump breast. "Why else wouldn't she
sell? $100,000? She killed somebody, that's
why. And he's buried there!"

We reminisced then, about the house in
Yonkers, long into the evening. And my father-
in-law's paintings, hanging on those elegant
wood-paneled walls, seemed suddenly mysterious
and full of life.

CANTO XV
(AS YOU LIKE IT!)

"Siete voi qui, ser Brunetto?"
[Inferno, *XV*]

The phone rang. Colin stared at the ceiling above his head, where an unsuspecting moth had landed in the two-day old web he had seen in the making (and given his gracious blessing to, in his decision not to use the broom on it). The moth fluttered its powdery wings in a desperate effort to free itself, then flattened deeper into the mesh--the effort to extricate itself having taken its toll. Watching the trapped insect, his hands behind his head, his desk chair tilted back against the black wall his mother despised (he had painted it one Sunday when his parents had gone out for the day), Colin toyed with the idea of withdrawing his protection and freeing the moth. He would have to free the web gently so that it would cling to the broom without damaging the moth. He would cut around the spot where the insect had landed, loosening the threads that held it captive. Would it work?

He came down on the front legs of the chair with a thud, ready for action. But just as suddenly his determination collapsed. What right had he to be so arbitrary! The web had come into being because of him--had he not given his tacit consent?--and there was a certain priority of loyalties to be considered. Should he destroy that two-day production simply on whim? He leaned back again. Tough luck.

The phone was still ringing. He picked up the receiver with a touch of dread, his eyes still riveted on the drama above him. It was his mother.

"I was about to hang up. Where were you?"

"I was just coming through the door--"

"Are you managing all right? Do you have what you need?"

"Yes. I got some things. But I eat out." It was always better to lie, he had learned. Besides his mother worried, but she didn't really hear anything. Just went ahead doing what she thought she should. Colin, she knew perfectly well, would have to fend for himself. The house had been closed for the summer. And, on those rare occasions when she and others came into the City, she knew exactly how to call in

31

emergency orders from the Gristede near-by.
She had wanted Colin to do just that; but,
naturally, he had not. His mother's efficiency
grated on him. And yet, there was no damn
reason for his feeling so hostile toward her.
She had made possible his own erratic behavior.
He always came and went as he felt, and there was
always everything he needed when he came home.

"Colin, dear, your father and I have to
come into the city tonight. That fellow from
Iran is coming. You know the one--we stayed
with him in Tehran last Fall, when your father
went out there about the oil."

"I wasn't with you--"

"Yes, but I told you about him. Anyway,
he's arriving at Kennedy around 9:30 and we
wired that we would meet him. Your father
called the office and Jerry will come out with
the limousine. We're taking a late afternoon
plane in. I have to make sure everything is
ready in the house. It's only for a few days.
We'll be taking him out to the Cape with us on
Tuesday. You won't mind too much, will you
dear?"

There it was again, that terrible guilt
he always felt, as though he were in the way,
somehow. He'd come home too soon, obviously.
Even before he actually got back, he knew it
had been perversely wrong of him. He could
have gone to a hotel. They need never have
known he was back in New York. And the error
had been compounded by not joining his parents
in the summer home on Cape Cod. Instead he
had gone directly to the empty house across
from the Wright Museum, screwing his whole
summer and everybody else's. But it's June!
(his mother had whined over the phone when he
had called them). You should be out here en-
joying yourself!

"Are you there, Colin?"

What had he missed?

"Honestly, I don't see why you don't
come out here. Jules is here with his sister.
And the Rattners. Jim and Toby were asking
for you last week, and oh, that fellow Clyde
from Germany, you know the one, his father is
with Interpol. You were thick last year--"

Frustration started again inside him,
like a slow poison in his guts.
His mother went on. "I don't understand
you. Why did you come back from UCLA so early?"
He had lied, but at the time his defenses
were down and he had done it badly. She had
sensed something more than he had volunteered.
It would be so much simpler, God knew, just
to go along. Why not go out to the Cape? His
friends were all there.
She meant well, of course. For a moment
he thought of complete and total escape. It
was still Friday. He could still walk to the
Chase Manhattan Bank and withdraw five, ten,
fifteen thousand dollars from his account (in
trust with his mother) and take the first plane
out somewhere. Tokyo. Australia. His passport was still good. Later he could write and
find an excuse his mother would accept. As for
explaining to others, she was very good at that.
The money would last him a couple of years at
least. Capri would be nice.
The receiver hung limply at his side.
He brought it back to his ear.
"...and the Eppners. With Judie." She
waited for his reaction. "Did you hear me,
Colin? Judie's here."
"She wrote she'd be there around the end
of the month."
"Well--?"
"Well? What? I'll get around to seeing
her. What's the rush?" They had made love in
the ocean one day, after driving for two hours
looking for a lonely spot. The water had been
cold and almost unbearable. Judie was fun.
Last year, he thought he loved her.
"...says hello." He was perspiring now.
"Who?"
"Ned. Ned Thompson. He suddenly popped
up the other day. Day before yesterday. I told
him you might be coming out soon. Wait a
minute--" Someone was there with her. "Bernice
just said that Ned left about an hour ago. Said
he'd pick you up and bring you out here. Do
come, darling!"
He closed his eyes. Damn. He would have
to think fast.

33

"Oh, darling, I AM sorry! But I didn't know he had left. I would have told him you didn't want anyone there--"

Fiercely and definitely not! What the hell!

"Look, I may not be here after all. I'm working on something and really, mother, I don't want to be disturbed. That's why I came back. I want to finish this work I'm doing before long. Then, maybe, I'll join you at the Cape. Damn, why didn't someone stop him from leaving?"

"But, dear, he came just to see YOU."

"O.K. Don't worry. I'll probably go to the Ontario Festival. I was planning to later in the summer, remember? I'll go now. It's no big thing."

"What about your work?"

"It's almost done," he lied fingering the telephone pad in front of him. He counted twenty slips of paper. "I've done about twenty pages. That's a good beginning." He could almost hear the sigh of relief.

"Oh, that's good. But I still think you should pack a bag and come out here."

"I'm going to Ontario, Mother!"

"Well, you needn't be sharp about it?!"

He counted to ten. Better cut the conversation short. They always went around in circles until he betrayed his impatience. He felt guilty enough without having to bear the brunt of having annoyed her.

The moth had stopped struggling. What do moths taste like to spiders, he wondered? Filet mignon? Fresh shrimp? Bass, just pulled in? Prawn from Florida? Ambrosia. Are spiders gods?

"...even if you're still there. So don't worry about it."

"Mother, please. Do what you have to do. Even if I'm still in the house, you won't have to do anything for me. Just tell what's-his-name that I'm busy working."

"Well...."

"So don't worry." He hung up. July and August suddenly loomed an endless infernal stretch of time. He must think of something. Keep running. Avoid the net.

He glanced up at the spider. Spider
and bees. What was he thinking? Oh yes. He
remembered dully something about sweetness
and light. What was so special about bees?
Moths, at least, abandoned themselves to something irresistible, were destroyed by greatness.
There was nobility in their desire for death
by fire. Even without a purpose. Slaves of
love, gravitating toward a Platonic mystery.
Surely there was something sublime about it--
spiders simply oozed out their own sticky greed
to lime the conscience of the king. Geometric
precision, symmetry, the whole complex illusion
of pattern did not excuse them from the fraud
they perpetuated on unsuspecting members of the
insect world. What he resented most, he suddenly understood, was the fact that the moth
would never have the chance to die in greatness.
     He would have to get out of the house.
It was the only way. If he didn't, he'd be
caught, trapped in his own web of frustration.
But whose fault was it? Who the spider, who
the moth?
     Brunetto Latini. Oscar Wilde. Ned.
     He had had a choice. (What if it happens
when you're eight or nine? What choice then?)
Or, more accurately, why should he be stuck
with the consequences, with the guilt and fears?
Not fears of discovery, although that too would
have to be faced sometime or other. Just...
fears. What? Had he chosen, really? Or was
it an unconscious Oedipal, subterranean pull
(curiosity?), the sense that he could see it
through. But it was different. Some nemesis
had been set into motion, regardless of his
intentions. Anyway, damn it, he wasn't an
eight-year-old. He knew exactly what it was
all about. What he hadn't anticipated was
this empty feeling of loss. That, he had
stumbled into.
     Had Ned stumbled into the same sort
of thing? It was hard to tell. The expert
and the novice are worlds apart. The distance
is closed between them only by the fact of
experience. Corruption makes us equals. One
looks back with a kind of perverse satisfaction
at the struggling victim making up his mind.

Hands off! (For the moment. Until a decision
is made or stumbled into.) Not a word. It's
a closed society. Mystery to be discovered.
Let him find his way into our castle. Besides,
no secret can be told to any who divined it
not before. The line kept going through his
head.
Judie would have been, O God! FUN.
They would have screwed every morning and
afternoon, lying naked in the cave by the water,
out near the lighthouse. Judie would have--
would never have understood. But then, she
would never know. Ned had known about THEM,
though. He had smiled every time the two of
them had driven off. Hell, come along, if you
want to, Colin had laughed one day. I'll use
my imagination, he'd said. Judie had pretended
she hadn't heard.
Have you reached a verdict?
I have, your Honor.
Extenuating circumstances. Unintentional
act. Under the influence. Sheer innocence.
The defense rests.
And the verdict?
Shall I put out my eyes?
A fatal error, a tragic flaw, a mistake
in judgment, a stupid careless moment.
Are we to be accountable forever?
You're the judge.
I shall pass sentence, then. No
rewinding the clock back. No flying around
the world to find yesterday somewhere in the
magic circle of time. Solitary confinement in
the swamp on a blasted heath, in--
The phone rang again. The breathless
voice reached him across the blasted heath.
"Just got in."
"My folks are coming."
"There's plenty of room, isn't there?"
"I won't be here."
"What's the matter?"
"I'm going to Canada. I was just leaving
the house."
"Shit. What the hell do you think you're
doing?" There was a slight pause. "I'll go
with you."
"No--"

36

"Look, I have to talk to you. I'll be there in ten minutes. I'm down at Penn Station." He waited until the buzz came on again and then hung up. Exasperation tore into his stomach.

"Hell, NO!" he cried out loud, hitting the desk with his clenched fist. Pain hit him in return, a delayed reaction which shot up into his arm and shoulder. Slowly, he leaned back in his chair and rested his head against the wall, opening his eyes after a moment and taking in the objects in the room. The mahogany bureau he had bought on the Cape years ago and had insisted on taking back with him. The corner bar. The Arthur Miller photo he had had enlarged. The Barcelona poster and fraternity pictures. Ned was in one of them.

He glanced up. The moth had not moved. He rose and went downstairs to unlock the front door, leaving it slightly ajar. On the first floor, his mind made up, he entered his parents' bedroom and went directly to the high chest where he knew his father kept the gun. It was loaded at all times, but Colin checked it out to be sure. He took it back upstairs to his room, leaving his own door half open. Whoever entered would have to push it in further and that split second was all he needed. He sat down at the desk again and studied his position opposite the door. It wouldn't be hard. For a moment he toyed with the idea of writing a note to his father, but decided against it quickly. What would he say? The last great lie. He could see his mother trying to read between the lines, struggling for some meaning she could accept. No, it was better this way.

Downstairs, the doorbell rang. He could hear someone calling, going through the living room, the kitchen, the dining room.

"You sonafabitch. Where the hell are you?"

"Up here."

The giant shadow moved into the room even before the door was pushed ajar. A cloak of darkness over the earth. All the kings men

37

riding pillage across wastes, devastating
continents, raping, murdering, drinking
their courage into the night. Ripeness is
all. And the ghosts locked up in dev-
astated bodies break through the dust to
answer the call. Spikes in a crown of
light. A giant spider coming to its unexpected feast.
     There was no time for surprise.
     Justice, your Honor. And in the
last dim shred of light, some trace of
mercy.

KENSINGTON

The intervening years had been telescoped
out of existence, and his last visit was suddenly an immediate reality again. Soho on Soho.
Earl's Court on Earl's Court. There he was
again, Stephen Horst, looking at the same porno
on the newsstands, the same bulletin boards
outside the tube station, the same subtle
excitement making his body tingle.
"Dominatrix." "Male model wants work."
"Young girl seeks homework: 12 noon to 11 P.M."
"Rubber and leather for sale." "T.V."
Morbid curiosity, Freddy had called it.
The girl had not touched him, but he
felt her there. Boots in the summer? The
Dominatrix, maybe. Yes, there was a touch of
morbid curiosity in it. At least that. The
vicarious thrill of obscenity, humiliation, pain.
Looking down into an abyss at once inviting
and repelling.
Look Ma!
Try it! You'll like it!
Augustinian puppets in a beehive of
creaking beds.
As always, he indulged in the long pull
of anticipation, as though he would do it, after
all. Why not! Experience. Knowledge. He
remembered Father Casey at the seminary quoting
from the Confessions: "Experience isn't an
absolute value. The rapist has no peace until
he has experienced what it feels like to rape.
The murderer wants to experience what it feels
like to put his hands on a person's throat
and squeeze it. The thief--"
The girl nudged him with her full breasts.
He could see the nipples hard and big under the
thin jersey blouse.
Freddy had said to him, in one of his
petulant moods, that he should have gone on to
become a priest. Damn Freddy. He remembered
everything Stephen ever told him. They had
been walking in Soho, where Stephen--as usual--
had been studying the pictures in the windows:
various nudes in all conceivable positions.
Exasperated and embarrassed, Freddy had finally
blurted out: "You really think you're virtuous
because you look but don't go in, right? Well,
that's NOT virtue, damn it! Virtue means

41

passing by these places and not wanting to look,
even!"
"That's stupid!"
"You're stupid."
"I'm curious."
"Ah. The great answer to all big and
little questions." Stephen had smiled an obscenity, but Freddy had not risen to the bait.
"Trouble with you is, you're still a
priest at heart. You've never gotten over it.
Deep down inside you're still an Augustinian...
but you let yourself be pulled in every direction. No determination."
He'd been right, in a way. Twenty
years ago his vocation had been a certainty.
What had happened? He wasn't sure himself.
Sex had triggered the decision. The drive was
overwhelming. And when he had started to
indulge he felt it was hypocritical to go on.
Father Casey had talked with him many hours,
but Stephen decided it was too late to do anything about it. Or was that simply an excuse?
Somewhere extremes meet, he had rationalized
at the time. Would they?
He was too possessive, Freddy. But
his only real friend. It was Freddy who should
have become a priest. Of course, he would
have hated being called a manqué priest. He
saw himself as a Socratic skeptic, evolving
his own self-righteous rules of conscience, a
ready-to-be Hamlet. Self-made, self-reliant,
self-contained, and fully responsible for all
his actions. But Freddy was Presbyterian.
As usual, he had waited too long and
the decision was made for him. The girl had
moved down the street. He saw her walking
slowly, her long black hair moving like a
soft carpet with each step. He realized he
had not seen her face at all.
Yes, sex intrigued him. The fact of it
was overpowering. It always crashed upon him
unexpectedly, enveloped in a thick mist.
Nothing was ever very clear afterwards. Only
the sounds, the movements, the obscenities, the
cries, and sometimes the scars to prove it all
had actually happened. Even with Frances it
had been like that--although those experiences

42

now were few and far-between. In retrospect,
it had always been...a kaleidoscopic noise.
Powerful, loud, leaving behind...insatiable
morbid curiosity. Still, he had never
experimented. For some reason, he had kept
away from homosexuals, from the kinds of
sex advertised on the bulletin boards he
was now looking at. Why? He could never
explain it adequately to himself, although
he always had an answer for Freddy. Perhaps
the normal experiences were already too
much for him. How could Freddy possibly
understand? Freddy was lukewarm about sex.
"Once a week," he had told Stephen in a
rare burst of confidence. "Nothing
terribly exciting...."
  "But you enjoy it?"
  "Sure. But I enjoy lots of things
that way. I love green lasagna and malt
Scotch, but I don't go into ecstasy over
them." He and Betty had too much else to
distract them. Four children, a big house
which needed constant attention, Saturday
nights at the faculty club, picnics with
neighbors, bridge and Sunday brunches.
And, of course, Freddy had his teaching,
his papers, his trips to conventions and
conferences, his books. He had already
written five--all of them top-notch studies
in his field. No problems for Freddy....
He had not been created, like Stephen, for
the pleasure of the gods, the supreme
ironist, self-deprecating and apathetic
about important things. The wit.
  "It's a gift," someone had said to
him once admiringly, when he had lashed
into a pretentious critic at a party. "The
lowest of the arts," a girl he had known
had tossed out, years ago. What was her
name? Katherine. Kitty, yes. Kitty Cervo.
Kitty Deer. They had joked about it. He
had liked her. She was clever and good-
looking. He could not tolerate stupid
women. The gods had punished him, of course.
They had given him...Frances. Stupid,
nagging, dumpy Frances. The supreme irony.
  The lowest of the arts. Kitty had

43

probably been right. Last time he had been
in Kensington, he and Freddy had passed
workmen carrying long metal tubes into the
station. He had gone up to them impulsively
and commented with a perfectly straight face:
"Carrying tubes into the tube, I see."
The tired workmen had been surprised, then
irritated. One of them had turned away. The
other had taken in Stephen's neat suit, white
shirt, carefully selected tie, and for a
moment he hesitated. "Another comedian!" he
had finally blurted out in his heavy Londonese.
Freddy had been embarrassed.

There it was. Had he been aiming for
this particular pub? He couldn't be sure...
but he realized with a start that he wanted
desperately to see Dave again, the carpenter
with whom he had drunk beer almost every
night for three months when he had last been
in London doing research for his book at the
British Museum. Once Freddy had joined them,
but he had not liked Dave. "Keep away from
him. He's capable of anything. And he's
a homosexual."

"How do you know?"
"There's a look about them--"
"You're guessing."
Freddy had been angry with him and
never came back to the pub.

"He's got a wife in Delaware," Stephen
had volunteered once.

"That doesn't mean anything. I know
several who have children. So what?"

He glanced at his watch. Five past
nine. Still early. The place wouldn't
start to hum until ten or eleven. He walked
in. Nothing had changed. It was a large
pub, nothing like the beamed cozy places he
was so fond of. This was more like the dives
on the Bowery. But the clientele was a
combination East Village, singles-bar, and
local Irish saloon. Soon it would be full
of hippies from the neighborhood, homosexuals,
old timers, locals, and slumming tourists who
somehow found their way there--God only knows
how--and came in for a few minutes to drink
one beer and to breathe the stale excitement

of the place before going back to the Strand
Palace or the Waldorf. He had been relieving
himself on the sidewalk, his friends forming
a close circle around him. Stephen smiled,
remembering.

He drank a Bitter, scanning the faces
around him. The young crowd had not yet
taken over. There were a dozen or so old
men sitting at the far end of the room, a
few couples, one girl asleep in a corner
booth, three small groups of workmen at
the bar. Well, he had all night. Frances
would not arrive until tomorrow. He was
still on his own!

Last time, Kitty had been with him.
God, they'd been good together! Nothing
like it had ever happened to him before.
He had been ready to throw everything away--
what was his job worth anyway? He could
always teach elsewhere. And Frances--she
wasn't worth considering, even for a moment.
She meant absolutely nothing to him. Never
had. The marriage had been a necessity into
which he had foolishly allowed himself to
settle down. "You're weak," Freddy had said
to him once. But life had been a kind of
punishment from the start. Why? "There's
always a reason," Kitty had insisted. "We
choose to be what we are. Even when we do
nothing, like Hamlet." Well, he had done
the "right thing" and had married Frances.
But the conditions he had set up so firmly at
the time were forgotten as loneliness set in
again. Sheer inertia had taken over; life
had dragged on, and in the process he had
fathered three children. It had not been
his decision at all!

Kitty could have changed all that.
With Kitty he had almost come out of it.
He would have, if--

He had wanted Kitty. Wanted her all
the time. They had never had enough of one
another. For the first two months, they had
spent entire days in bed. Sex had been
overwhelming...and unlike all his other
experiences. He had never enjoyed a woman
more. Once--early in their relationship--

45

he had stayed with her all night and they
had not made love at all. They had talked
and he had recited whole passages from Dante
and Keats. He had explained freedom and pre-
destination and made her memorize Spinoza's
phrase, "Freedom is insight into necessity."
He had wanted to prove something....

And their last night together, she
had finally come to his flat. Hadn't she?
Why couldn't he remember? The whole thing
was one of frustrating confusion. But she
had been there! Her cologne was in the air
the next morning. He could smell it now,
just thinking about it.

The memory came crashing back on him
and he felt the piercing stab of despair
once again. It had shattered him, her dis-
appearance. He had tried convincing himself
that she was just another bitch, after all,
but even as the thought came back to him,
he knew it was a lie. Everything about her
had been genuine. She had clung to him,
affectionate and passionate. Everything he
had ever wanted.

Dave, of course, had tried to steal
her away. They had been a faithful three-
some for the entire time he had frequented
the pub. Was it really four years ago? It
seemed so intense and immediate still...and
just a few hours ago, he had not even remembered her name!

"Sensuous hands," Dave had said.

"She's marvelous!" Stephen had
whispered to him, just loud enough for
Kitty to hear. She had smiled, looking
away, as she drank her Scotch.

"You lucky bastard," Dave had blurted
out on another occasion, when he was well on
the way to getting drunk. "What the hell
have you got that I haven't?"

"The lowest of the arts," Stephen had
laughed.

"Up yours," Dave growled.

"Arts, not arse."

"What the hell do you know about arses?'

"Try me."

"You wouldn't know how."

"Intellectuals are notoriously good fuckers."

"Is that a challenge?"

"Mary Astor wrote in her memoirs that the best lover she ever had was S. J. Perelman."

"He was a Jew."

"What the hell has that got to do with it?"

"He was circumcised."

"Is that supposed to make it better?"

"Only one way to find out--"

"You just don't grasp the subtleties of the thing--"

"Fuck the subtleties. What you grasp is--"

"How do you fuck the subtleties, I wonder?"

"All you do is talk, talk, talk. And all the while you know damn well that the only thing that counts is sex. Come off it, you bastard!"

"Trouble with you is you don't talk enough about it!"

"I'll beat you at it every time!"

"Sure, if you go about it like--"

"--I mean, you're such a fucking liar! You want it all the time, even now, while you're spouting all this shit." He grimaced. "Gimme, gimme, gimme, that's you. But you fight it even as you grab." He turned to Kitty. "Darling, tell him to shut his fucking mouth," and he leaned across Stephen to kiss her. "I'd be so good to you...you know I would!"

"For a couple of days. It might be fun," she had replied.

"What makes you think I couldn't, if I really wanted to?"

"Habit. It's the hardest thing to cure."

"You make it sound like a disease or something." Kitty had laughed.

"Habit and temperament."

"What's wrong with my temperament?" He had turned away irritably and gulped down his lager.

"Nothing. Only it's not mine. Or

47

Stephen's." Dave had put down his beer mug
and stumbled into the men's room. He was
gone a long time, and Stephen followed him
finally into the washroom. Dave was leaning
against the open window. In the harsh light,
he had taken on a purplish hue.

"Are you all right?" Stephen had
taken his arm, but Dave moved away roughly.
He turned on the tap in the washbasin and
soaked his head. "What are you mad about?"

"You and Greta Garbo!" He shook the
water from his hair, like a dog, and then
plastered down the loose ends with his hands.
Stephen had burst out laughing, but something in Dave's expression stopped him
abruptly. A sudden constraint came over him.

"Well it is funny!"

"Everything is a huge joke to you--"

"That's not fair!"

"All's fair, my friend." He moved
toward the door, Stephen at his heels.

"Dave, you're not really angry with
me?" He saw the other's mouth twitch and
his eyes narrow into a squint, but it was
gone before Stephen could even begin to
define the emotion.

"Hell, no." He burst out laughing,
his whole body shaking convulsively. He
put his arm around Stephen's shoulder and
they walked out together back to the bar
where Kitty was waiting. "But don't say I
didn't warn you. Cocks and cunts. Cunts
and cocks. That's all there is, friend.
And don't you forget it!"

Later, he and Kitty had helped him
back to his room and put him to bed. He
had scribbled a note, his head swimming.
"Sticks and stones will never break my bones,
but Bitter with Scotch will surely wet my
crotch." It had been his last night in
London. Crossing the room he had stumbled,
and when Kitty caught him he had embraced
her and kissed her passionately. His last
night with Kitty. Why couldn't he remember?
A sudden panic came over him as it had that
morning when he woke up to find her gone.
What the devil had happened? He still

couldn't believe she would go off without a
last word, a note, some sign....They had
planned to meet regularly after he had settled
Frances and the children in Oxford. But when
he had tried to reach her, she had moved.
The place was beginning to fill up.
He stared at the loose-breasted girls. In
a few years they would look like cows, but
right now he had to admit they were very
desirable. Kitty had had small breasts. It
had not mattered to him, but she had said
on more than one occasion: "You're disap-
pointed."
"Don't be silly. It's you. That's
all that matters."
"It would have been better though if
they had been bigger."
"Or if you had an extra one."
Once she had sat cross-legged on the
bed for half an hour, stroking her nipples
to make them large.
Did he really expect to see her again,
tonight?
He recognized Dave the minute he strode
through the door, pushing his way through the
crowd at the door. He looked the same, except
that he wore glasses. Stephen waited until
he had found a spot at the bar, then approached
him from behind and poked him in the ribs.
"Why you bastard! What the hell are
you doing here?" His broad face lit up in
recognition.
"Waiting for you--"
"I never expected to see you again!"
"Not without glasses, anyway."
"Yeah. Didn't have them when you
were here last time. There's irony for you.
The professor doesn't wear glasses, and the
carpenter does. What are you doing here?"
"Professors move around, you know."
"Well, it's a rotten coincidence. I'm
leaving for the States tomorrow! Stephen
raised his eyebrows in surprise. "Yeah.
Going back to me woman. We patched it up.
She was here for a couple of weeks last month.
What the hell, it's worth another try, I
guess." He pulled back his head and studied

49

Stephen. "Jesus, it's good to see you!"
"I'll be in London the whole year
this time. Found a flat on the Old Brompton
Road. My wife comes tomorrow with the kids."
"Too bad. How about that, Balls!"
He gulped his beer.
"Think you'll settle down there?"
Dave shrugged. "Who knows? I can
always come back. Why worry?" He mused,
"After all the rows we used to have...I
can't believe it myself--"
"It's a switch, all right." Stephen
motioned for two more beers.
"But I'm not getting any younger.
And there's good money for my trade over
there." He picked up the beer. "To the
wives." He emptied the glass.
"Trying to get me drunk again?"
"Ha! Doesn't need much trying, if I
remember rightly." He stopped abruptly
and a strange expression came over his face.
"Are you...alone?"
"Until tomorrow."
"Can't escape them, can we? It'll be
a strange experience for me. I have't felt
married in over twelve years. We were together only a year and a half. Oh, I saw
her once in a while. She came to England a
few times. I guess she's a permanent part
of me, whether I like it or not. Can't
escape...."
"You can. I can't. Oh well, why
cry about it?"
"Why bring her here if..."
"Needs a holiday, she says. What the
hell. It's easier not to fight it at this
stage of the game." He felt the trap closing
in. Why in damnation had he agreed? Only
a few more hours of freedom. Dave must have
read his thoughts.
"Hell, the other things don't last.
They're never the same again."
But Kensington was the same. And his
instincts--
"--new friends. New adventures. It's
the only way."
"That was special." He took a deep breath.

"We say it every time."

"Don't be cynical--"

"Me? Cynical? Why you son-of-a bitch you!" He put an arm on Stephen's shoulder. "You were the one who was always bugging me with your intellectual crap!"

"Does she come around at all?"

"Here?" Dave dropped his arm. "I haven't seen her since that last night we were together, the three of us."

Something churned inside him. Why would Dave know any more than he did? She had never gone back to her apartment after that last night. And when he had written, the letters had come back unopened from the post-office, address unkown.

"You didn't really expect to find her here tonight, did you?"

"Is that so odd?"

"After four years?"

"Why not?...You're here!" Dave looked away. "I mean, why is it so impossible?"

"And if she did walk in, what would you do, eh? What did you do last time?" Stephen did not answer. "Look, your wife comes tomorrow. And I go back to mine."

"Why?" Why was it so compelling for him to set up house with Frances when there was absolutely nothing between them? He hadn't touched her in over a year.

"We need routine to survive."

"Not that kind. That's death."

"Then get out of it."

"I would have. Back there. I wanted to, and was ready to do it."

"Hell you did. You wanted it just the way it turned out. You talked about getting out of it, just as you're doing now... but what you really want is what you have." It all sounded vaguely familiar.

"You're wrong."

"You indulge up here too much." He touched his head.

"I can't run after your kind of excitements...."

"You do, in your subtle way."

"Mine are pale, believe me."

"You think they are--" He took out
a package of cigarettes and offered one to
Stephen.
"I've stopped."
"Go on!" He studied him through a
mist of smoke. "I'm afraid to ask what
else you've given up!"
"You wouldn't believe me if I told
you."
"Come on!!! You're not telling me
you've stopped fucking!" Stephen said
nothing. "You must be joking!" Why was
he admitting this to Dave? Even Freddy
didn't know. "What the hell for?"
"The computer inside me has been
programmed in a very special way. It's no
good, damn it, unless--"
"For God's sake, you're not impotent!"
"It just won't work if it's not
right."
Dave shook his head and let out a
long slow sigh.
"You're full of surprises!"
"A glutton for punishment--" He
remembered Kitty saying that once. Dave
eyed him speculatively. "Go on, say it--"
"Nothing." He leaned on the bar.
"It just doesn't make sense."
"Last time...I knew right away.
Everything was right. From the very beginning."
Dave turned away brusquely. He
avoided Stephen's eyes and kept his face
averted when Stephen spoke again.
"I really loved her. And yet, earlier
this morning...before I started out--you
won't believe this--but I couldn't even
remember her name. I hadn't thought about
her in months...years. At first, it was hard,
but then...I just slipped back into...routine."
He was suddenly very much annoyed with himself.
"That was stupid! Not even remembering her
name! What the hell is the matter with me?"
He stared at the ceiling, his heart pounding
with frustration and anger. "Stupid!
Incongruous!" He drank quickly. "Oh, hell."
"She wasn't worth it!"

"Didn't even leave a note." He was restless now. "I will have a cigarette, if you don't mind." His hand shook as Dave lighted it for him. "That last night...you know...I conked out, too. I don't remember anything after we put you to bed. And the next morning she was gone. Oh, she'd been there, I'm sure of it. Her cologne was still in the air. She had been with me, I know it."

"You can't be sure--"

"You and I quarreled, remember? Well, you know, that business in the washroom?" Dave looked down at the bar and traced patterns on the wet surface. "Then we took you to your place and put you to bed." He waited for some sign. What? "The point is, I don't remember a damn thing after that!"

Dave squinted at him. "So, what's there to brood about? We all get drunk sometime or other." He loosened his shirt. "It's getting hot in here."

"The strangest part is, I had no intention of coming here. I mean, I wasn't even thiking about it. I just found myself...headed this way. And now...I guess I had to come to find out...."

"What there to find out?"

"I'm not sure." But something was nagging at his brain.

"You put me to bed. That's it."

"Well, if I passed out at your place, who took me home?" Dave gave him a hard look.

"Damn it, how should I know! You probably staggered back, with Kitty."

"It IS hot in here." His shirt was soaking wet. "Let's go outside for a few minutes." They picked up their beer mugs and elbowed their way to the door. The place was jammed now. Like the last time they had been there. Nothing had changed.

Outside Stephen took a deep breath. "I'm sorry, Dave. But it's been preying on my mind, I guess, without my knowing it. Funny how it all came back to me suddenly, when I came here. I guess I never really got over it. I loved her--"

"Oh, come off it! Anyway, it's four years ago." He walked to the curb and spit. When he came back his face was hard and unfriendly. "Chalk it up to experience, whatever you like to call it."

"You never saw her again?"

"Crap! What is this? You indulge your secret self and then take it out on me!"

"What's that supposed to mean?"

"Just that." He turned away, but Stephen grabbed his arm.

"What do you mean, I indulge my secret self?"

"What you don't remember won't hurt you."

"Tell me!"

Dave strolled away and came back slowly to where Stephen leaned against the stone wall of the building. "Okay. So you don't remember. Leave it at that, why don't you."

"Hell, no!" He moved forward and faced Dave. "You know something and you're going to tell me!"

Dave laughed, "God, you're thick." He tilted his head to one side and watched Stephen for a few seconds. "Okay. So you were drunk and passed out."

"And then what?"

"Then I woke up." Stephen waited. When Dave spoke again his voice was cold and impersonal. "Don't give me that shit. You weren't out. Nobody could carry on the way you did and be out. Sure, you were drunk, but not out."

"What happened?"

"It lasted all night, sweetheart. You should have gone home after leaving that note. Not let me find both of you stark naked on the floor in my room...I mean, that's tempting, right? And then Rudy came in with his friends. We had a ball. All of us. You too, pal." Stephen stared at him. "You enjoyed every minute of it. God, I've got to hand it to you. I thought I was oversexed, but you beat me, you son-of-a-bitch." He turned to spit again, this time against the wall. "I told you, nothing but cunts and cocks. I warned you, remember? Anyway, why brood? She wanted it like all the rest of us...Yeah, we took you both home. She must have left later." He caught Stephen's expression. "It happens every day, baby. Like I said, chalk it up to experience. Pity if you really don't remember. You were awfully good for a novice...."

Stephen reached out savagely and grabbed Dave's shirt, but the other pulled away with a deft movement. "You bastard!" He lashed out, sending Dave's beer mug into the street, the beer spurting over the pavement in a wide golden arc. His own glass splintered at his feet. Dave spun around and pinned him against the wall.

"I don't want trouble, see?" It was a hoarse whisper. He waited a few seconds and then let him go. "You asked for it. It was your doing, every bit of it." His mind swam and he felt himself going limp. Pictures struggled into focus. Were they porno shots he had seen in Soho? He heard Dave's voice again from a great distance.

"...no different from all the others. And you. Nobody baits me, pal! You wanted to be proved wrong, but I'm the expert, see? You couldn't win." He moved backwards. "It wasn't me who started it. It was your party, all the way. When she started to leave, you forced her back....Like I said, nothing but cocks and cunts." He turned and strode back into the bar.

Stephen straightened up slowly, still leaning on the wall. The crowd was thick in the streets now, but nobody seemed to have taken notice of the quarrel. Just another brawl. He crossed over and headed toward the Kensington tube. The sign was lit over the entrance. ALL NIGHT SERVICE. They laughed when he had told Kitty about the prostitutes who lingered conveniently under it. He staggered up to the rail outside the entrance to the station. They were all there, an assortment of all sizes, shapes and colors. Nausea gripped him and

he doubled over, his head low on the rail.
When he opened his eyes, he scanned the faces.
Several were very young. He moved forward.
One of the girls approached him and spoke,
but his head was throbbing and he couldn't
make out what she said. It didn't matter.
Whatever she wanted. He stumbled beside her
all the way back to his flat. The pictures
in his mind were clearer now, although his
body ached.

Three on a mat. Smoke and groans.
A feast of hands. Sweet stickiness. Incense.
Black.

Once in Soho he had seen a huge Negro
walking down Carnaby Street, a small blonde
keeping pace beside him. They had seemed
purposeful and detached. Stephen had looked
back until they disappeared around the corner.
Days later, he had gone into a movie and there
they were, the same two, on screen, pulling
and twisting in the studied lust of experts.
Dave had had a black roommate once....

All's fair....Cunts and cocks....Black
and white. Sometime in the night he woke up
and vomited. Later, in the thickness pre-
ceding dawn, the opening lines of a poem he
had once memorized came back suddenly, weaving
in and out of his consciousness:

Lo! Thus, as prostrate, in the dust
I write my heart's deep languor and
my soul's sad tears

He fell into a fitful sleep at last and saw
himself walking the cold deserted streets of
Kensington in threadbare slippers. In his
dream, a girl stepped out of a doorway and
stood in his path. It was Kitty.

He started to speak, but the sounds
stuck in his throat and his lips would not
move.

She was wearing white boots and a
poncho. Her hair was full and thick and wet
over her shoulders and down her back. She
nodded toward the doorway from which she had
emerged, waiting for some sign.

Stephen stood rooted to the spot.
When she finally walked away, he wanted to
scream. He felt the sound of it inside him,

56

bursting to get out. It surfaced finally,
like a knife stab, and he woke up in a pool
of sweat. Beside him the girl raised her
head in surprise. Her eyes were bloodshot
and her large mouth hung loose. He reached
out and gripped her breasts until she squirmed
with pain. When she began to moan, he pulled
her out of the bed and forced her on her knees
on the floor. Then, suddenly, he became aware
of rain outside the window and raised his
head, listening. He heard the door click
shut. When he turned around, the girl was
gone. He put on his slippers and found his
raincoat under the tumbled covers of the
bed. Outside, it had turned cold and the
rain was coming down hard. He walked quickly,
his head down, to Kensington Station. Under
the shelter of the entrance, he looked
around. It was almost dawn. Two drunks were
sitting on the curb, resting against each
other.
 Across the street he made out the
door. It was set inside an archway, probably
the entrance to a mews. He peered into the
darkness, trying to make out if anyone was
standing there. All he could see was the
faint glow of the lion's head knocker.
 He turned up his wet collar and waited.

THE FUNERAL

Three weeks. She should have gotten used to the idea by now. But on this crisp April morning, outside St. Jude's church, Helen waited for the hearse to arrive, utterly convinced that it was all a mistake. It wasn't wishful thinking. It wasn't a fixation. It wasn't the effect of traumatic shock. She simply was convinced that Dick was not dead.

And yet, the pain and terror and grief thrust upon her three weeks earlier with the bare announcement of the fact over the telephone had persisted and grown. This too was strange, since what she grieved for was not the death of a friend but the utter certainty that for reasons she could not begin to understand Dick had chosen to make them THINK he was dead. It wasn't fair. He should have given his friends some clue, some sign of his intention.

Another car had pulled up in front of the Church. Behind her Fred gasped:

"Look! It's Mary!" She watched with a kind of fascination as the grotesque figure was lifted carefully from the front seat of the car. Fred had gone quickly forward and was helping to adjust the portable wheelchair which someone had taken from the trunk of the car. Hal settled his wife carefully in the chair then straightened the hat which in the maneuvering had settled at a ridiculous angle over his wife's eye—that is, the black patch she wore to hide the hole where once her right eye had been. Fred leaned down to greet her. Mary twisted her face upward, fixing her good eye on the people hovering above her, forming—Helen could hear even at a distance—the guttural sounds which passed as words, since the woman's larynx had been removed. Five—or was it six?—operations; and there she still was, wanting desperately to live and succeeding—while Dick—

They had all been classmates in graduate school at Columbia. Before Mary's cancer at twenty-four. Before Fred had married his sexy waitress and moved out to New Jersey. Before... this.

She could smell death. It rode up slowly

to the tiny group waiting in front of the
Church and came to a halt halfway up the block,
leaving behind a trail of decaying odors like
a slow-spreading stain. Or was it just the
flowers?

  Someone tugged her sleeve. It was Fred.

  "This is Laura Platzek." The woman's
eyes were red and swollen, but her thin face
was very pale. A thin, balding man held out
his hand. "Mr. Platzek." Who were these
people? But she knew, of course. Laura
Platzek. Dick's wife. The wife he had married
so that she could enter the States. The wife
he had promptly let go, according to some
private agreement carefully worked out before-
hand, and left free to marry as she pleased.
The wife with whom he had never lived and
whose family had become a part of his life.
It all made sense, but--

  "...good friends. He seemed happy--"
Mrs. Platzek turned away and blew her nose.

  For Helen, Laura Platzek had never
really existed until this moment. Dick himself had never mentioned her; but Fred and
Ralph had known, of course. She had learned
about it only the day before, when Fred had
called to tell them of the funeral arrange-
ments and had mentioned the Platzeks. She
had felt a twinge of resentment. But a
loner like Dick, she had told herself, never
would confide the details of his personal
life to others. Fred and Ralph were his
oldest friends. They had known one another
for over fifteen years. She glanced at
Mr. Platzek. Had they ever met, the two
men? But of course. They must have. What
was it like, she wondered, eating dinner
with the man who had once been your wife's
husband?

  She caught herself sharply. What
nonsense! Why shouldn't the men be friends?
It was a bit unusual; but if it hadn't been
for Dick, Laura would never have entered the
country and would never have married her
present husband. Surely there was a logic in
it somewhere. The whole business was--

  There was a commotion near the Church

door. The priest had come out in his vestments and was talking animatedly with the undertaker. Mrs. Platzek and Fred went over to join them.

A third car had driven up, and she saw Ralph and Dr. Hadad in the back. A third person got out of the driver's seat and looked over the top of the car at the group near the Church door. Ralph saw her and came over.

"I knew there would be trouble!" There was something womanish and a stubborn pettiness about him, but even his perpetual frown did not detract from his good looks.

"What do you mean?"

"The undertaker said something to Fred yesterday about health regulations."

"What does that mean?"

"But Laura insisted on a Mass." The group was dispersing. The Platzeks went to their car and got in. Fred came back to them.

"Father Doyle is mad as hell! He went in to change."

"What's happened?"

"They won't take the body into the Church."

"Why not?"

"Something about a health ruling."

"That's what Ralph said."

"So we go directly to the cemetery instead."

"That's ridiculous!" said Ralph. Fred was suddenly all efficiency.

"No point arguing about it. We tried." The priest had come out again in his street clothes. "I guess he'll be riding with the Platzeks." He watched as the priest entered the first car. "You ride with us Helen. Unless you have some other plans."

"No."

"Good." He led her to the car in which Ralph and Dr. Hadad had driven up. Dr. Hadad held out his hand.

"It's been a long time." He got out as Helen walked around to the other side. "Where's your husband?"

"In bed with the flu. Oh, he's all right. But I don't think he should go out

63

yet. He still has some fever." Fred helped
her into the car. Dr. Hadad followed her, and
Fred settled near the window on the right.
"Are you comfortable there?" He had long legs.
        "It's O.K." The driver had gotten
back in, and Ralph now came to sit beside
him. He half-turned in his seat as the driver
started the car.
            "It's been over a month, you see."
            "Doesn't make sense," Fred said. His
voice was unnaturally loud. He was deaf in
one ear. "The crate was sealed hermetically,
wasn't it?" He leaned across to Dr. Hadad
and stared at him. "There shouldn't be any
odor, should there?" The cars had lined up.
Theirs was the last one. In front of them
was another full car with friends from Columbia.
Mary and her husband were in that one. The
first car was the Platzek's blue Pontiac.
And up ahead was the hearse.
            "Have you two met?" Ralph suddenly
remembered. Helen shook her head.
            "I don't think so." The driver
glanced around.
            "I think I met your husband once."
            "Bob. Bob Gorman. He lives in the
house where Dick lived." Fred settled back
in his seat.
            "Well, there shouldn't be any odor!"
            "Maybe not." Dr. Hadad shrugged. "The
point is they can insist, as they have. The
health ruling is clear."
            She could feel death stirring in the
pit of her stomach, pricking her eyes with
the almost unbearable pressure of tears.
She had cried enough, God knew. But it was
no easier to hold back the tears now than it
had been when Fred had called that bright
sunny Saturday morning three weeks earlier,
breaking into a late brunch and a happy mood,
to tell them that Dick had died in Marseilles
of a heart attack. She twitched uncomfortably
in her seat remembering how she had thought,
unfeelingly, hearing the disbelief in her
husband's voice and words: It's Mary. They've
found another cancer. And how a cold guilt had
gripped her when George had put down the phone

and said simply, with a catch in his voice, "Dick is dead."

He had been about to sail back to the States, they had learned in bits and pieces. On the same merchant ship on which he had signed up a year before. Where had he been? It had been the longest absence she could remember in all the years they had known him. He had said to them, the last evening they had been together: "I should be back next April or May." And they had both reminded themselves all through that cold February and March that soon Dick would be back. They were impatient to see him again. It had been too long.

"Are you comfortable there?" It was Fred, leaning across Dr. Hadad to speak to her. She had burrowed into the corner and had been staring out the window, her head resting against the glass pane.

"Oh, yes. Fine." He was pleasant enough, Fred. And reliable in emergencies. But George had grown wary since the time that Fred had started to tell them, around coffee one night, all about his girlfriend and their sex life together. He had already decided to marry her, and George took exception to the stories. "You don't talk that way about a woman you're going to marry, damn you!" And if it hadn't been for Dick there would have been a terrible fight. Fred had never forgotten the incident. And George avoided Fred whenever he could.

"Remember to keep in line," Ralph was telling Bob. "You can go through the red lights. Just stay behind the other cars."

Death was right in front of them, covered with decaying flowers. When they turned a corner to feed into the Expressway, Helen caught a glimpse of the large unpainted crate lying the full length of the hearse. No, not quite the full length. It was a large crate as crates go, but...surely not large enough for that big body.

"...legal permission to open the crate. It's the only way it could have been done." It was Dr. Hadad's deep voice. Ralph turned around to him.

"Well, why the hell didn't she get it!
At least we'd be sure!"

"Oh, don't start that again!" said Bob
beside him.

"The poor woman has had enough on her
hands," said Dr. Hadad. "When you consider,
she has done more than her share. Try putting
yourself in her place. She hadn't seen him
in over two years. Suddenly she gets a call
that he's dead. In Marseilles. She could
have left it at that."

"But she's his heir!"

"SO? That's everything?" Fred followed his own track.

"You're stupid, you know that?" Ralph
wouldn't let it go. "I'm talking about SOME-
BODY doing the right thing."

"And you're an imbecile!"

"What Ralph meant," said Dr. Hadad
quickly, "is whoever was authorized to do so
should have gotten the crate opened for formal
identification. But," he went on quickly,
leaning forward to claim attention, "I don't
think it would have been wise."

"Why not?" said Ralph, pursing his mouth
to match the deep frown.

"Many reasons."

"And the two sisters in Poland.
Shouldn't they have been notified?"

"They will be."

"The point is," Ralph persisted with
his characteristic doggedness, "everything is
wrong. No Mass. We're all told to meet at
the Church and then no Mass. What kind of
funeral is that?"

"Good God, Ralph! She wanted it more
than any of us! You saw what happened back
there. Father Doyle was furious. But you
can't fight City Hall."

"But to find out the last moment, with
everyone there, waiting to go in? It just
doesn't make sense."

Bob glanced around. "Why brood about
it? It's over."

"Keep your eyes on the road," said
Fred.

"Bob's right," said Dr. Hadad. He

pronounced his words carefully with the meticulous emphasis of a cultured foreigner. But Ralph went on stubbornly.

"After all, one expects to enter the Church. At least for a blessing in the vestibule. Something!"

"Damn it, she tried, I tell you!" said Fred, hitting the back of Ralph's seat with his open hand.

"The whole business is weird, if you ask me," Ralph went on, settling comfortably in his seat and looking straight ahead.

"Nobody's asking you," said Fred with a touch of sharpness, as though he had heard it all before.

"Well, I'M not satisfied!" He turned around abruptly. "And neither are you, in spite of what you say! You're wondering about the same things. What we're all wondering. If there isn't someone else in that crate up ahead!"

"What shit!"

"He was a healthy man," Ralph went on with studied calm. "A man like Dick doesn't just fall down and die at thirty-nine." He swung around. "My God, Fred, you can't really think--"

Fred sighed. "We've been all through that, Ralph. Let up, will you?" He glanced at Helen. "Facts are facts. And that one--" he pointed to the hearse "speaks for itself!"

"Wrong! It does NOT speak for itself. And you know it. You're not sure either!" In the pause that followed, he crossed his arms and settled back in his seat. Bob glanced at him and shook his head.

"He had no history of heart disease, did he?" Helen ventured at last. Ralph sat up quickly and turned to her.

"There! You feel the same way, don't you!"

"There WAS an autopsy in Marseilles...." It was Dr. Hadad.

"That's what we were told."

"Facts, Ralph. Facts," said Fred quickly.

"And no one saw the body, right?"

"Whoever performed the autopsy did.
There are documents to prove it," said Dr. Hadad.
"A stranger. Is that a proper identification?" Ralph sensed his advantage in the
pause that followed.
"O.K. So none of us here saw the body.
But you can't open a casket after three weeks."
"He was embalmed, wasn't he?"
"Health regulations," said Dr. Hadad
simply. "Even if he had been embalmed, it
would have been impossible. Unless there was
some doubt about the manner of death, or if
the identity of the person was suspect. Then
it's a police matter. There's another thing."
They waited. "That crate up ahead doesn't
contain a body. Just...remains. The body is
not intact."
"You mean it's chopped up?"
"Oh, come off it, Ralph!" Fred's
exasperation finally surfaced.
"Well, it's important to me! Why should
the body have been chopped up? I mean an
autopsy doesn't mean the body gets cut up into
pieces, does it?"
"I didn't say it was cut up into pieces,"
Dr. Hadad replied. "Three weeks is a long time,
that's all."
"No, you said more than that just now."
"Why did she have it brought back at
all," said Bob suddenly. "It might have been
better just to have it buried over there."
"I'm not so sure," said Dr. Hadad. "At
least, this way, we KNOW. We're here and we
can see he's dead."
"But we CAN'T, DAMN IT! That's just IT!"
"Oh, shut up, Ralph!"
Dr. Hadad stroked his chin. "I think
she did the right thing. They have a plot.
And she may know something we don't. After
all, as we said earlier, she WAS his heir.
Whatever he left her--and it probably wasn't
much--that's not the point. As his heir she
would want to do this last thing. I can
understand it."
"And the sisters in Poland?"
"What about them?" Fred countered. "Did
you expect them to go to Marseilles and claim

the body? He hadn't seen them in over twenty years."

"And the plot in the cemetery is not for outsiders, is it? Platzek bought it," Ralph went on, following his own line of logic. "You all know I'm right. You just won't admit it!"

"Good God! Right about what? What are you suggesting?"

Dr. Hadad put his hand on Fred's sleeve and shook his head.

"Don't," he said.

"But he's crazy."

"Here we are, following that crate up ahead," Ralph went on, tapping the dashboard with his long finger, "and none of us, not a single one of us in this car, really believes that's Dick in there." He turned around to see the effect of his words on the others. "THAT'S what!"

Dr. Hadad frowned for the first time. "That's utter nonsense, Ralph." He glanced at Helen. "And morbid."

"He's dead, all right," said Fred.

"Are you absolutely sure?" There was a long pause. "The whole thing is fishy--"

Helen leaned forward. "That's exactly how George and I felt--" The others said nothing. Dr. Hadad glanced down at his hands. Fred leaned his head back and closed his eyes. Ralph turned to her eagerly, waiting to hear what else she had to say. She was suddenly embarrassed. "What I mean is..." her voice trailed off. "George was saying--well, he led such a strange life!"

"It's all quite improbable," said Dr. Hadad, as though he had read her thoughts.

"But why?" she asked gently. "How much do we really know about him?" She plunged ahead. "What did he do for a living? He was away for months at a time. Almost a year this last trip. Well, maybe he WAS on a merchant ship. But why? Last time it was Hong Kong. Before that it was India and Australia. Korea. Africa. Why? Couldn't it have been a cover for--"

"I give up," said Fred suddenly.

"We're all crazy."

Dr. Hadad took her hand. "He's dead.
One way or the other, he's not coming back."

"Well, yea. I can understand that,"
she went on lamely. "But it DOES make a
difference knowing that...." She stopped.

"Does it?" Dr. Hadad peered at her.
"How?"

Was it really just her imagination?
Not wanting to believe the obvious fact and
looking for some other explanation--howsoever
absurd--to cling to? Some scrap of mystery
to hang on to?

"I don't quite know. It's...well, we
used to kid him about his secret work.
About being an agent. Why couldn't it be
that?" Dr. Hadad looked away.

"It was just his manner. You mustn't
even think it."

"Well, it's not impossible," said
Ralph.

"He was a very strange man," mused
Fred, as though a hole had been bored into
a secret recess and the contents now
trickled out. "We didn't know very much
about him really...."

"This sort of thing leads nowhere.
And it can be...very unhealthy." There was
a note of sharpness in Dr. Hadad's voice.
"You musn't indulge in it."

"This," said Ralph in a loud whisper,
"would have been the perfect screen. That
crate up ahead with something in it. Oh,
sure, there's a dead body or remains up
there. But it's not Dick."

Dr. Hadad looked straight ahead. "We
don't know anything. You're opening up a
Pandora's box to no good purpose."

Helen touched his arm. "But, Dr. Hadad,
if he's alive--"

"If he's alive, if what you're thinking
is true--and I don't for a moment subscribe
to it--then we would do him a great disservice
probing this way."

"You're right about that--" said Fred.
Even Ralph seemed taken aback.

"If he is still alive and under cover

as you're suggesting Ralph--" he waved the
other down and continued "--then the last
thing he would want is for us to suggest it."
"Do you really think..." ventured
Fred. He had great respect for Dr. Hadad.
"I don't think anything. I will not
think about it. I simply...accept." He
passed his hand over his brow. "Even if this
is a way out, and the whole thing is preposter-
ous, of course, but even if it were true...we
won't ever see him again. That's all there
is to it."
"So you know what I'm talking about--"
said Ralph, somewhat subdued.
"Oh, I KNOW!" said Dr. Hadad. "But
I don't like it one bit. You're not helping
at all."
Fred looked at him. "But you HAVE had
doubts--"
"Perhaps. But it doesn't matter. And
I refuse to talk about them."
Ralph sighed. "I wish it were that
simple for me. We were such good friends.
Fifteen years is a long time. He was almost...
a brother. Why shouldn't I brood about the
possibility of his still being alive?"
"Because if it's really true, he
wouldn't want you to."
"You know, there's another possibility."
They had forgotten about Bob. He leaned back
now, his eyes on the road. "He might have
been...wiped out. In that case--"
"But the result would be the same!"
said Dr. Hadad impatiently.
"Wait a minute now. Let me talk. If
he was killed, then I think we have a right
to bring it out into the open."
"And just how would you do that?"
"I suppose the body could be exhumed,"
said Ralph hesitantly.
"You're absolutely mad!"
"Well, you asked how. That's how.
It's been done."
"But there's no suggestion of foul
play!"
"Dr. Hadad is right," said Fred. "Even
if it were foul play, we could never find out.

Besides...it might be dangerous."

"That's exactly my point!" said Dr.
Hadad. "If he was killed as an agent--and
I'm NOT saying I go along with this crazy
notion--but if he was, just suppose he was.
Do you think our raising dust like this is
the right thing?"

Why not. Why not. Why not. She
recalled the scraps of information he had
tossed them over the years in his impersonal,
detached way. Once in a great while he would
recount his adventures back in Poland as a
boy. In Chile, when a dog saved his life
during an earthquake, by pulling him away from
where the earth suddenly gaped wide behind
him. What had he been doing in Chile? And
during the war in the British navy, later in
South America, seeking men who had taken
refuge in far off places and had never been
heard of since. At one time he had had three
different passports.

"...on the wrong track altogether."
It was Dr. Hadad. "I believe he was simply
working so that he could come back and finish
his work at Columbia. Why not leave it at
that?"

"Because there are too many loose ends!"
"He would have said more had he wanted
to."

"You're right about that," said Fred.
"So why are we probing this way?"
No one answered. "We're all in a kind of
daze about it. But it doesn't warrant this
sort of talk."

"Anyway," said Bob, "if he were really
forced to go under cover, we'd never run into
him again. So the end result is the same."
He glanced around. "I mean, he would even
get plastic surgery done, if necessary. We
wouldn't recognize him if we saw him again."

"You've got a point, there," said Fred.
"But I would like to KNOW just the
same," said Ralph in a dramatic whisper. "He
was my best friend. And I would like to know
that he's alive, damn it, and NOT DEAD!" He
turned brusquely in his seat.

Make it true, she thought. Her head

was swimming and her eyes were clouded over
again. Had she loved him? Was her frustration
simply the realization she would never touch
him again? See him again? Talk to him again?
Yes. What else? And yet, there had been
nothing physical about it, no remote suggestion
in her mind that they would ever become lovers.
Ralph felt it too, she was sure. How could
there be any kind of love in the usual sense?
Love is possessive and exclusive. None of them
felt that way about him. He was the great god
Pan, emanating mysterious rays that drew
others to him like iron filings to a magnet.

Had she read more in his glances than
she should have?

Ralph's voice reached her as from a
great distance. "--had someone deliver money
to Hal about six months ago! Money he had
owed him for five years or more. As though
he knew he wouldn't be coming back...at least,
not for a long long time."

"You admit, then, that my construction
is sound."

"In a way, yes. I never said you were
wrong. I simply feel--crave--more for myself.
But, if he really had a plan of that kind,
you're right: he wouldn't want us to make
waves."

"He was at Columbia for how many years?"
Fred picked up the same line. "Ten, twelve,
whatever. On and off, sure. But always take-
it-or leave it. Just for kicks. And then,
suddenly, last year, he decided he wanted a
degree. He had almost enough credits. In
fact, he did have enough. All he needed was
some papers and he had to take some exams.
He actually took about three. And he was
writing papers." He turned to Ralph. "Did
you know about that?"

"Of course, I knew!" Ralph replied
irritably. "He was coming with me to three
courses last year."

"He came to George about helping him
finish two papers," said Helen.

"Maybe he waş trying to tell us something...." Fred was suddenly alert. He
glanced at Dr. Hadad. "It's not far-fetched--"

73

"What? What was he trying to tell us?"
Dr. Hadad was non-commital.
"That he was not going to die. He
may have known something like this might be
in the works, and he wanted us to know that
it was just a...ruse of some sort."
"What's the point of that? I'm
listening." Dr. Hadad was firm.
"We could hope, at least...."
"So." Dr. Hadad finally turned to
look at him. "If you really believe that,
why don't you just let it go. Let's assume
he is indeed alive somewhere. He may come
back someday. You see, I listen. I hear
your argument. In that case, he is telling
us: don't say or do anything, just hope."
He paused, then went on. "He's telling you
that either way, alive or dead, you musn't
count on his coming back. No matter how
probable it may seem. And perhaps, in some
desperate way, he was saying that he'd tried
his best to fix things so that if he ever
did come back, nothing would be lost. On
the other hand, he could also be saying: "I
knew it was a long shot. If I make it back,
well--then, we'll talk about it perhaps. If
I don't make it back, you'll know that it was
a hard assignment and that the odds were
against me."
"Dead but not really dead. Is that it?"
"Yes," said Dr. Hadad simply. "And we
should leave it at that."
"It does make a difference, you see,"
Helen heard her own voice, a disembodied sound
coming from afar.
"If you wish to think of it that way,
go ahead. But no waves."
"Did he say something to you before
he left?" Ralph had turned again in his seat
and waited expectantly. His voice was natural
and his eyes direct.
"Of course not!" said Dr. Hadad. "But
if you think a minute. What else could all
that you have said here today possibly mean?"
"We like to feel that he might still
be alive, after all," Helen volunteered quickly.
"It DOES make a difference!"

"Believe me, it's no good thinking
about it. As far as I'm concerned, he's dead."
     He was right, of course. Any way you
sliced it, Dick was to all intents and purposes,
quite dead. She thought suddenly of Pearl,
the shy myopic clerk in the reference room
of the Library, who had read so much in his
kindly attentions and in his casual invitations
to have coffee in the afternoons. Dick had
mentioned her once. What would Pearl say when
she learned about him? She had written him
hopeless love poems and had thought--who knows
how many hopeless thoughts!
     She recalled with a twinge that she too
had written him a poem once. She had shown
it to him one evening when he had stopped in
to visit with them. He had laughed at "garlic-
flowered words" and for weeks afterwards had
asked about his breath. "Aren't you flattered?"
she had asked impishly when he had finished
reading the poem. "How many other women have
written sonnets to you?" He had thrown back
his head and laughed. "I don't know about
sonnets...but poems? A few." "Oh?" "You
don't think it possible?" "Oh, it's not that.
I just...no, I don't think it possible. Not
this kind, anyway. A work of art." "Well,
yes. Not like this one." He had given her
a long look. How much had he understood?
     They had reached the gates of the ceme-
tery. The three cars came to a stop on the
narrow path just inside the grounds. The
hearse had gone on to the very end of the path.
The ruddy-faced undertaker had gotten out and
was saying something to the people in each of
the cars. When he reached theirs, he leaned
inside the driver's window.
     "Please stay in the car until the coffin
has been carried to the grave and placed in
position. I'll signal you." They waited in
silence while the crate was taken out and
placed on the special device that would lower
it into the ground after they were gone. Then,
at the signal, they all got out and walked to
the yawning hole and listened to the brief
prayers. Father Doyle seemed upset and spoke
hurriedly, almost petulantly. When he was

done, he walked over and said something to the Platzeks, then walked slowly by Mary's wheelchair as she was taken back to the car, bending down once in a while to speak to her.

The funeral director quickly opened a large brown envelope and took out some wilting rosebuds which he distributed to the rest of the group, instructing them each in turn to approach the grave and throw the flowers on the crate. When it was all over, they were led back to the little path while the men in overalls, who had been watching at a distance, came forward to prepare for the lowering of the crate into the ground. Helen stopped by Mary's car to greet her. She was already installed in the front seat. Hal was sitting directly behind her. He got out when Helen stopped to talk to them.

On the way to Bob's car, she said goodbye to the Platzeks, who were just then returning to their Pontiac. Theirs was the first car to turn around on the narrow path and head back towards the gate. They all watched in silence as the car went by, the woman small and pale between her husband and Father Doyle.

Back on the Expressway, the men debated about where to have lunch. It was close to three. They finally decided on Sloppy Louie's, a fish place on Fulton Street, and after much coaxing, Helen agreed to go along. They would drive her back to the house, later.

The place was empty except for two other people, sipping coffee. There was sawdust on the floor and the tables and benches were raw and bare. The food, she remembered afterwards, was very good--but she was never able to recall what exactly she had ordered. Her only memory of that part of the afternoon was Fred's stories about their escapades, Ralph's account of how Dick baited him about his idol, an anthropology professor--a tall, lean, dull man, who was fond of reducing all social phenomena to "x" and "y" equations on the blackboard--and Dr. Hadad's reminiscences about their visits to Egyptian restaurants that featured male belly-dancers.

Back home, she looked in on her husband, who slept uneasily, the covers wrapped tightly around him like a cocoon. She went back into the living room and picked up the brass Indian tray Dick had given them as a gift on his last visit. It was badly tarnished. She took it into the kitchen and cleaned it carefully with Noxon, several times. After she had finished with it, she stood by the kitchen sink, staring at the intricate geometric patterns cut into the metal, until she heard George calling from the bedroom.

A TAPE FOR BRONKO

The name finally began to register on my second day in Belgrade. Perhaps it was the massive back of his neck and the solid squarish head above it that made me hear "Bronko." It was weeks later that I got it straight: Svonko. But by then, my first impressions had taken root and the original name stuck.

Coming off the plane, I was too busy greeting my hosts and the government representatives who were waiting for me to notice Bronko. Official invitations were extended for the next day and my itinerary for the month-long tour was thrust into my hands. There was the usual confusion of gathering luggage, finding my passport, meeting people, disposing of members of the party in the various cars sent out by the embassy for the drive back into the city. My eyes were heavy and my whole body ached from the long flight from New York and the two-hour stopover in Paris; but knowing my friend E.B. (who was my official host in Belgrade), I knew I would have to stay awake into the small hours of the morning.

It was only when I had finally settled back into the embassy car, with my escorts, that I became aware of Bronko. My first impression was through a tired mist. Bronko at the wheel was like a block of granite. I noticed his hands first. Like the rest of his body, they scarcely moved, even as he turned and maneuvered. They were large hands, rather pudgy but not at all soft. There was something formless about them—or so it seemed at first—a grotesque enlargement of a baby's fat fingers and thick round wrists. But this impression was, I decided almost immediately, wholly misleading. He was all muscle, and I suspect he could have killed a man with one solid blow.

Everything about him looked solid and tough. The innocent Chevelle he drove' for the embassy took on vibrations of greatness under his touch; and when he opened up on a clear stretch of road, the car took on his characteristics and became an artillery

tank. The Chevelle in action was a monster;
they were made for each other.

He was not a bad driver. On the
contrary, he drove with disciplined economy--
which I, for one, appreciated and admired--
but the rules were his own. Like most non-
Americans at the wheel, he was highly compe-
tent in a kind of creative recklessness which
is the trademark of many European drivers.
They are artists at the wheel, I had learned
from a two-year stay in Naples; expressionists
in a neglected medium. In America, Bronko
would have withered away driving at 65 miles
an hour along the Long Island Expressway, in
a Cadillac or an Olds 98. The very thought
seems blasphemy. He drove the 5-gear
Chevelle at breakneck speed on level stretches,
with a nervous intensity that betrayed
itself only in his chain smoking. How
he enjoyed weaving in and out of caravans
of slow-moving trucks and vans, racing
up blind curves on the wrong side of the road
to pass a presumptuous 600 as it puffed
along, trying to maintain its dignity!

Through all this, he maintained an
external calm which inspired confidence. No
matter what he did, the car somehow responded
to his arrogance, cowed by the energetic
display of authority. I learned, from the
very first, to relax and enjoy it.

The next day, on the road to Novi Sad,
he pointed out the cellophane-wrapped wreaths
which hang on trees to mark the spot where a
traffic fatality has taken place. The only
irony was in the smile I resisted. He was
altogether too simple and wholesome to indulge
in hidden parallels.

He was to pick me up again two days
later, when my business in Novi Sad was done.
On the appointed day, he arrived three hours
early. I was waiting in the lobby of the
Varadin Hotel for my luncheon guest, Professor
N., when Bronko strolled in. I was flustered.
What does one do with a borrowed chauffeur
who arrives three hours early? He sensed my
predicament. "Don't worry. I wait."
I asked him if he had had lunch. "Don't worry."

He nodded reassuringly and started to move
away. I followed him. "Have your lunch, then,"
I persisted. "Don't worry. I eat." I couldn't
tell if it was present, past, or future tense.
Later, I glanced back and saw him propped up
on one of the stools in the miniature bar of
the Hotel, sipping a beer. As I went in to
lunch with my companion, I saw Bronko come in
after me and sit down alone near the door. I
smiled in relief, and he gave me one of his
slow, reassuring nods. I felt guilty about
wasting his time. Much later, I wondered if
he had paid for the lunch out of his own money.
I hope not.

    I learned his name by slow stages: not
Bronko but (I thought) Svenko; not Svenko (I
finally was told) but Svonko. But, as I said,
by that time the name Bronko and the image
that emerged were indissolubly one. I could
no more relinquish that first name than I
could betray the impressions that had evoked
it. I called him by his right name from then
on, but it was only a concession to formality.
Inside I still said "Bronko."

    The morning I left for an extended trip
through southern Yugoslavia, Bronko was there
to see me to the airport. I was to be away
about ten days and, since Bronko had to be on
hand for the embassy people in Belgrade, I was
to have another temporary driver for that time.
I was all packed and just about ready to leave,
when I remembered a tape recorder my host had
offered to let me use on the trip. We tried
it, but the batteries were dead. Bronko disappeared without a word and returned in a
matter of minutes with new batteries. They
weren't any good. He left again and came back
with a new batch. God only knows where he got
them at seven in the morning! When the machine
finally responded, he put his hand on my
shoulder as if to say, Did you really think I
would let you down?

    I was so grateful for his gruff
attention and so taken with his quiet compe-
tence that I placed the recording machine
away with exaggerated care...and completely
forgot my passport. It cost me an extra day

in Pristina, while frantic calls were made to
the embassy in Belgrade. In spite of the in-
convenience, I felt strangely pleased: a
small price for Bronko's selfless optimism!
Only later, as I settled back in the car for
the long drive back to Belgrade, did I remember that I had not used the tape recorder
at all. I was shattered. What would I say
to Bronko if he asked about it? I owed him
some sign of appreciation, some proof of
success. What could I possibly offer in the
way of an explanation?

A dozen projects flitted through my
mind, but none of them seemed worthy somehow.
I am certain that Bronko would not have really
minded if I simply said: "I didn't have a
chance to use it." But I felt that his
efficiency deserved a better conclusion. A
journal? A travelogue? A short story?

I was jolted back to immediacy by the
slamming of brakes and realized that I might
not get a chance to say anything at all! M.,
who had been assigned to seeing me safely back
to Belgrade, had been forced to a full stop
as he attempted to pass a huge van. I cursed
under my breath. If only Bronko were there!
Oncoming cars flashed their lights in warning.
My driver squeezed back into his lane, and I
sat up in my seat, stiff with tension. In my
mind's eye I saw all the black wreaths that
had accumulated in my memory, the battered
wrecks that had been left on the grass near
the road somewhere near Pristina, all the
black-edged notices on the hundreds of trees
we had passed, the grim warnings to motorists.
I thought of Bronko again, the unconscious
primitive, whose movements were always under
control. My perverse imagination pictured
the notes, cards, and manuscripts in my brief-
case strewn over the road to be gathered up
eventually by the peasants, arranged into a
display (with my name in the middle), a black-
edged reminder to others--the whole work of
art pinned to the nearest tree. I thought of
Bronko pointing out the spot to some other
American guest.

M. didn't know a word of English, but

my guide sitting beside him heard my
sarcastic comment and answered that his
friend "was not a frustrated racing champion
but simply a 'professional driver.'" The
boast (so it seemed) set my antennae
quivering. It was unfair, perhaps, but I
determined to shatter his illusions. I tried
to tell myself that the poor man was just an
ordinary human being, likeable enough in
ordinary circumstances, and really no worse a
driver than so many others on the road. I
couldn't bring myself to believe any of it,
though. In the end I gave up trying to
redeem him.
        He was a short, thin, wiry man, with
a tremendous appetite. I can still see him
eating heartily, his head bent low over the
plate. He read the sports pages of the
papers the same way, hunched over the print
as if he somehow had to eat the words in order
to grasp their meaning. These moments of
rest, innocuous enough, simply added fuel
to my irrational antipathy. Still, I would
try to picture him at such moments with his
wife and children at home, sitting at the
head of the dining table, lord of his home.
Surely he must have some redeeming qualities!
At lunch in Sopocina, I watched him wiping
his mouth after a full meal and laughing with
his friend--my guide. "He says," my interpreter informed me, "that he requires very
little in life. Only three things--good
food, good wine, and women." M., laughing,
repeated the phrase in his own language,
confident that it was a good joke. I smiled
weakly and asked my guide if his friend was
married. My last illusion depended on the
vision of wife and babes waiting patiently
for him at home. No, he wasn't married.
At this point, I gave up trying. M. was a
boor and a lousy driver.
        A portion of my resentment, I must
confess, was that I saw in the poor man...a
competitor. "Professional driver" indeed!
Should I tell him about MY experience driving
alone through the Brenner Pass in January?
Of the blizzard just outside the Pass, when

I lost my host's car and had to trust to sheer
instinct (not being able to make out the signs,
even) to reach Innsbruck? Of the marvelous
control of the Neapolitan drivers, who always
gauged distances to the last second and somehow made the most outlandish maneuvers seem
perfectly natural? Of the--" I remembered
that there was no possibility of real communi-
cation between us and gave up. What I wanted
to say could not be said through an interpreter.
I would have to find some other way to crush
his confidence.

Actually, I had very little time to
brood. He was so preoccupied with his per-
formance as a "professional driver" that he
constantly missed things in the road and kept
hitting bumps and other obstacles, swerving
suddenly to avoid them and never quite succeeding. The worst part of it was that he
loved to talk. He and my guide would carry
on long conversations for stretches at a time;
M. would turn to look at his companion as he
spoke (which accounted for the near-misses),
and all this while the radio blared. He had
turned it on at the beginning of the trip and
kept it going all the way back to Belgrade.
I had debated whether to have him turn it off,
but--perversely--decided against any show of
irritation. He would never understand it, and
moreover, I was curious to see him in his own
"element," without any attempt to crush his
natural instincts.

After a wrong turn near Sopocina (it
had cost us an extra hour on a dirt road, with
peasants in black staring at us as we invaded
their domain), he stopped abruptly to ask
directions. In so doing, he swerved to the
right and landed in a ditch two feet deep.
He backed up precipitously, while I held my
breath expecting the muffler to be ground
loose. His confidence was maddening. My
last tense moments came just outside of
Pristina, when he passed a bus and remained
on the other side of the road until an oncoming
car flashed its lights and, in panic, moved
to the side and came to a complete stop on
the shoulder of the road. I saw the shocked

face of the other driver stare at us as we
zoomed past. My guide said something to M.
--with a trace of impatience--and he moved
back into the right lane sharply.
     Behind the wheel, he literally
squirmed, hunched over it as he hunched
over his plate and newspaper. He took the
turns with his right arm raised high above
the wheel, elbow out, tracing a sweeping
half circle. Invariably, he would smooth
his hair with his left hand at these moments,
or scratch his left ear. When he passed
other cars, he would announce his intention by straightening up in his seat,
squirming, and slowly negotiate the characteristic half arc high above the wheel.
When he came alongside the other vehicle,
he would look over with a supercilious air,
slowing down somewhat to relish the triumph.
If we passed a woman on the road, even a
young peasant woman carrying a load of wood,
he would look back appraising her over his
shoulder. Cows were a special target: he
would frighten them into confusion by blasting
the horn at least a half a kilometer away,
and not slowing down for a second. These
eccentricities had a certain fascination,
I admit.
     But, bumping along the narrow mountain
strip between Solonica and Pristina, watching
M. attack the thin macadam edge between the
rising cliff on the left and the unprotected
drop on the right, my mind focused again on
Bronko. He had FLAIR! His instincts were
reliable. His bulk behind the wheel, reassuring by comparison. I suddenly decided
that I owed him some sort of thanks. And,
as I brooded revenge, I remembered the tape
recorder. What better way to acknowledge
his superiority than to record my impressions
of other drivers encountered during the trip?
Not that he would understand. He would
probably never play it even. But I owed it
to him.
     M., of course, would be the central
target. But there were others...like the
driver who picked me up in Dubrovnik in the

Mercedes, to drive me to Mostar and Sarajevo.
He was a tall good-looking French-Italian
Slovene, with a thin moustache, who insisted
on talking for the entire length of the trip
--seven hours at least! His broken Italian
necessitated constant rephrasing of platitudes. There was no escape. And there was
the university "assistant" who, insisted on
taking me to the...but that's another story.

SAN FRANCISCO JOURNAL

AUGUST 28. My mind is riveted on one thing.
I woke up out of it (dreaming its idealized
version) and got up to smoke a cigarette. It's
now 4:28 A.M. I can see the water from Joan's
living room. She's asleep. God, how she can
sleep! It's not human. She turned when I got
out of bed, then went right back to sleep again.
I can never go back to sleep again.
I've got to work my way to it each time. So,
I'll scribble out here until the light comes
up and I can wake Joan up to talk. She hates
to talk. Still, she does listen.
...It's scary, how, lately, I fall into
dreams which are extensions of my waking life.
I dreamt of R. earlier. He was beautiful.
And kind.
I will NOT write to him until he answers
my last letter. I've made up my mind. (What
if he doesn't write again?) What I mean is,
words have wings. Once out, they'll always
be there to bear witness against you. One has
to build a screen, a...scrim. Create distance
between one side and the other. And just
enough light to enable others to discern some
vague familiar shapes. That's the best way.
I WILL write. That way.
Dear R.
We look into eyes and the soul leaps
out. Or, rather, the god of love leaps out
and stabs us--to use the language of the
stilnovists (who have never been surpassed in
this). Not even Donne comes close. They were
precise and inventive in an easy way. And always inspired. Who else has done justice to
the poetic challenge of finding precise
physiological equivalents for psychological
states--particularly the phenomenon of love, of
FALLING IN love? Nothing like it anywhere else.
And always tender, quietly sad, but full of
kaleidoscopic insights, light on light. No,
not even Donne.
What is this thing?
After that first stabbing sensation,
paralysis, shortness of breath, quivering
sensations in the limbs, dizziness, a long

pain in the stomach and complete disorien-
tation. All of this described in the most
lyrical way and matched at every turn by
psychological difficulties: the inability
to face the beloved and that first wild
moment of recognition, fear of betraying
one's feelings, willing suspension of
freedom, complete obsession with everything
connected with the beloved.
Love forces the beloved to love in
return. That's one way.
Later, all of this becomes cliches.
Dante's description of Beatrice as a divine
apparition is fresh and infinitely appealing
in its multifaceted simplicity. But with
the Renaissance poets and the metaphysical
poets, rhetoric takes over more or less.
The secret lies in describing the moment of
DISCOVERY. Dante's account is forever fresh
because every lover recognizes that magic
moment when uncertainty turns into conviction.
The time of sweet sighs. That's the first
part of it. Then, WOW! Right between the
eyes. It's the wonder of it that Dante
describes. That first wild moment. The
transparency. Light on light.
So here we are on the threshhold of
a mystery. A new life. I suppose I'm
trying to read the X-ray image of the internal
landscape all lovers suddenly see--the
contours of the soul.
What sort of computer can trace
internal landscapes? Or is it simply
RECOGNITION that makes some of us poets
and artists?? Whatever it is, only they
can describe it. And lovers are all
potential poets.
(The clouds look very solid. German.
Everything has been stored away in heaven,
or washed, or thrown out.)
Dante would say: And then we came
out into the open again and saw the stars.
(Inferno)
And: Thus prepared, we moved on--ready
to batter our way to the stars. (Purga-
torio)
And: I was one with that magnet that

moves the sun and the other stars. (Paradiso)
     Which, very simply means: We walk out
of nightmares and regain sanity looking out
at the sky and the stars. And, having re-
gained some sort of composure, we are strong
again, eager for the long trek. And, if we
don't look back, we'll finally touch the sun.
     Something like that.
     Hamlet would say: This distracted
globe....
     Hegel would say: The aesthetic ex-
perience is the arresting power of beauty;
and at its peak, that experience becomes the
worship of beauty, which then is translated
into the metaphysical probing of Beauty (which
is Truth which is God). The poet, the priest,
the philosopher trace different meridians to
the same orange peel.
     Aristotle would say: God is thinking
(subject) thinking (verb) thinking (object):
pure ACT. Self-knowledge, self-sufficiency,
absolute freedom.
     Spinoza would say: Freedom is insight
into necessity.
     Pao Lu Tsi would say (after Confucius):
We're all gradually settling into pure matter.
Some will be half-baked, some well done, some
rare--or so it seems to rotting eyes. The
resurrection has already come and gone. One
way or another, it's working in all of us as
we follow the path of hell and come out again
to see the stars. What we do then is something
else. Virgil saved Dante. Who will save me?
     "Ees a paradox!"
     I'm convinced, you see, that it's all
happened before in much the same sequence...
only reversed. The Platonic year (36,000 is
about right) is about the span of history.
We're approaching the end of the forward
sequence. Then, the mirror image in time
backwards to the beginning again. But which
is real and which is the image? Are we
really moving forward, or have we already
turned on our axis and moving back to something?
     Amoret in the House of Busirane.
     Francesca in the unquiet eternity of

romantic love, forever restless with her lover beside her. Why? Why? Why?

The worst part of it is that even if he were here right now, there is a limit to how much we could say or do. Oh, making love is nothing. It's over and done with soon enough. And, oh God! the large desire which comes after that! It's frightening. What would I do with him if he WERE here? I don't know. But...I want it.

Sorry about that.

Where were we?

A distant view seen through trees and hedges, provoking thoughts about infinity. We drown in it, like the poet says. Still, I don't know that I would prefer to be a golden bird in Byzantium. I'd rather perch, alive and sad, on the scarecrow who is Christ, the hook-nosed Jew, despised and deserted by his own. I like the paradox in it--but then, I'm perverse! Still: mere truth. Christ (light and love) is shut out forever from Light and Love (God). Isn't that the price he paid? Why doesn't any one like to say it? That Christ is in Hell? "My God, my God, why hast Thou--?" I don't rationalize about these things. As Pascal said, they disappear if you do. And without paradox, what's it all about?

Christ teaches nothing, he simply IS the reaching out, the profound paradox which the faithful full of grace call, naively, mysteries. Why not?

Dogmatic statements may or may not follow all this. That's not important. What's important is this: The Church is the rock of despair on which Peter (the literal critic, the weak cautious lover who betrayed his beloved not once but three times...and was saved) builds the Church.

Who is saved? Who is worthy?

"Quisque amat ecclesia, tantum habet spiritum sanctum."

Something like that. The measure of grace within you is the extent of your love for that Rock of Nothing and all the bricks and mortar that have been carefully placed

94

over it to hide it from the children's view.
For the poet, the Holy Ghost is inspiration.
For the lover-priest, it's grace.
For the philosopher, it's insight into darkness.
But all this was clear, wasn't it, on Grouse Mountain where, in the winter, you don't touch ground. (There I go again!) It was marvelous going up in the railcar, sensing an imminent mystery. That was the most perfect moment. Before certainty. Before words. Before touching. "Il tempo dei dolci sospiri." Sweet. Sweet. Sweet. Even Dante faints at the memory of it.

On Grouse Mountain, in the summer striped squirrels (Virgils in disguise) call the bluff and dare mortals to take the chair lift to the top (Dante's light bark at the beginning of Paradiso: Don't follow me there, if you're not ready!)

But, of course, it's summer and the ground is hard. No waters to cross. No cross to bear.
Still AUGUST 28. A predictable day. Coffee at 7:30. A new pot at 8:30, when Joan follows me yawning into the kitchen. How the hell can she sleep so much. She conked out at 9 last night, right after the movie began on Channel 5.

I showed her the letter from C.B. "I liked your poems. They're so full of energy, surprise, and dazzlingly lurid features, but also extraordinarily varied in tone and way of working."

"It's contrived," Joan said, attacking her coffee. I could have killed her on the spot. Instead I managed to spill some juice on her nightgown. She yelled bloody murder (it was a Kloss she got on sale in Bloomingdale's). I took the spot out for her with cold water.

"You might as well show me the rest," she said after a while.

I looked at her innocently. "What?"

"Oh, stop playing games! You know what!" So I took out R.'s letter and showed

it to her. She held it off (she'd left her
glasses in the bedroom) and started to read
it, sipping her coffee now. It was the second
cup, the one she really enjoyed. The first
was always a necessity with her; she always
drank it, no matter how hot, inside a couple
of seconds. She laughed and read out loud:
"'Your letters seem, are strange, quirky,
and memorable (but then so are you). Your
letters in a funny way are you.'"
"What's funny?"
"The first part is O.K. Tolerable.
But the second falls flat."
"He's not writing for posterity, you
know."
"Can you be sure?"
"Oh, go to hell!" I tried to get the
letter back, but she held on to it, pulling
away from me.
"He knows you'll save them--"
"It's the only one. How can I save
'them'?"
"Don't be touchy."
"Don't be a bitch!"
"Oh, for Chrissake! It's too early
in the morning for quarreling!" She studied
the letter some more. After a few seconds,
she looked up, wide-eyed. "Well, I mean!
What do you expect me to say?" She read out
loud again. "'Like most good poems, they're
disturbing.' I mean, really, he COULD have
thought up something a bit more original!"
"He wasn't trying to be original. He
said simply what he felt!" Joan can be ex-
asperating at times!
"Well, it strikes me as trite, if you
must know. Good Lord! Of course all good
poems are disturbing! They're supposed to
be. They're supposed to shock you into
awareness. How dumb can you get?"
I suppose there was some truth in what
she said because I grew angry. Joan went on
blithely. She was wide awake now. "'I like
your things enormously; your variety is especially impressive, .in that you're poet and
playwright as well as scholar-critic.'" This
time she didn't even try to be tactful. She

burst out laughing, doubling over with the
strain. "That's good!"

"All right. What's funny?"

"Scholar-critic. Don't you think so?"

"Well, I DO teach, you know. And write
articles."

"Hell, it's like the other bit. Trite.
No, it's worse than that. It's trite and
false. I mean--" she looked at me with an
air of innocence "you're a tolerable writer,
but hardly a scholar-critic! My God, you're
only 25! No one can be a scholar-critic at
your age! Not even Plato."

"What's Plato got to do with it?"

"Well, he DID say that no one should
write before he's thirty-five...and then only
if it's an irresistible urge. Like sex."

"You're impossible. And it's not like
sex."

"I'm being perfectly honest."

"Spare me that!"

"O.K." She was looking down at the
letter again. "THIS I like--part of it, any-
how. 'When you write about professional
things, your words are so full of you--your
inventiveness, your breathless rush of energy,
your indescribable grace--that reading them
leaves me quite shaken.'" She paused, serious.
"Yes, that IS good. The last part especially."
She handed back the letter. "There, you see?
I CAN be fair."

"Oh, hell!" I was annoyed.

"You're too romantic, I've warned you--
how many times? You're hopeless that way,
I think. Look, if Dante had sat down with
Beatrice and eaten a plate of spaghetti with
her, he wouldn't have had to pine away like
that."

"He wouldn't have written any poetry,
either."

"So what?"

"I can do without the spaghetti."

"Sure. And poetry doesn't make the
world go around."

"What world?"

Is it really all that? Why was I so
taken with your letter? My judgment is no less

keen than Joan's. Is it love that makes us
read mysteries in ordinary phrases? Or are
there mysteries that elude the possibility of
full expression and must be translated in
the loving exchange of memories? Is it the
"explication de texte" that we recognize familiar signs?
Still AUGUST 28. Joan has gone out for the
evening. She wanted me to double date with
her, but I told her: definitely not! The
last time I double-dated with her was a year
and a half ago, in New York. I had to fight
my way out of a bedroom on East 65th and
waited for Joan in the tiny foyer of the town
house where we had gone. She finally came out
at 8 A.M. I could have killed her.
        "Why didn't you take a cab back to the
house?"
        "I was worried about you!"
        "You're stupid."
        "You're crazy."
        "Anyway, why didn't you stick around?
It's good clean fun."
        "Because I don't like to be pushed
around. Or mauled. I don't do things simply
to fill up time. Especially not that. Because
I couldn't stand that creepy guy you were with
and I WAS worried about you. Because I don't
like casual sex."
        "Why not? You don't have hang-ups that
way--"
        "You're promiscuous."
        "You know the definition of promiscuous?"
        "Slice it any way you like. You ARE."
        "It means 'with anybody.'"
        "You pick and choose, I know. Like at
cocktail parties. You look around and set your
sights on that one or this one."
        "Promiscuous means 'with anybody.' Do
you see me hanging around street corners?"
        "Judas! Have you ever counted how many
you've had in the last six months?"
        "It's the attitude. Any good psycholo-
gy book will tell you that. You really ought
to get out of this rut you're in. You don't
even make an effort to meet people. What's
the matter with you?"

She had really tried. But the men she
met were not interested in HER. Oh, they were
interesting enough, some of them--and then the
overtures began. She was sick of it. So they
had fallen into a sort of partnership-- a
tacit understanding. Joan would not nag her;
and she, in turn, would watch over Joan. God
knows she needed someone to look after her.
Well, I've been chosen. She wants me to scold
her, I've decided. Like smoking. She wants
to give it up but doesn't know how to begin to
do it. Her will isn't strong enough. But then
...I have my own weaknesses, I guess. But the
important thing is that I am not angry with
her, ever. She knows that.
        No letter today.
AUGUST 29. Is love really touch and sweat and
all the rest of it?
        The mail has come. Same as yesterday.
Two bills, this time; an invitation to a pub-
lisher's party; a note from my sister in Phila-
delphia. I suppose I really should begin to
shut doors and turn locks. I don't want to
be caught off guard, pining for something
impossible. Look at the facts, for God's sake.
        Augustinian puppets (or Calvinist, or
Lutheran--doesn't matter) in a bee-hive of
creaking cells. Isn't that what it's all
about? Isn't that what one remembers best?
        Trouble is, sex is wrenched from us
while the appetite is still strong. But the
imagination is tired, and we've seen all the
dirty pictures. What's left?
        Review the Platonic sequence. An ar-
resting object; recognition; movement toward
fusion, identity. Finally, the baffling
frustration because it doesn't last that way.
One becomes two again. Blind mouths. The
silence of marble screaming toward light
under the sculptor's touch. If only one could
be molded into the shape of love, forever!
        Sure, there's Buddha and Zoroaster and
Aztec gods. Nirvana, small and large rituals,
the God who shouts, Moses the Supershmuck,
long-haired naked angels running across the
campus. But they all grow bald in time; and
then we study phrenology models and maps of

the brain, and trace the geography of the body
with cold fingertips. Blasphemies reverse
themselves in Hegelian antitheses. All is
paradox again.
 "I am a nerve o'er which doth creep the
else unfelt oppressions of this world." But
NOT Harriet's. Shelley was a bastard as well
as a poet.
 So we know. Does it help? Experience
is perverse illumination. The gift of the
ironic gods to their slaves. The result is
insufficiency, limitations, frustrations, in-
satiable appetites for a declarative sentence.
More! Followed always by "Basta! Basta!"
Heaven is the elation of the willing puppet,
love-addicted. (God knows I'm willing to be
a puppet that way. But then, why can't I
relax in it?) Hell is the clutching for things,
holding on to personality in the face of
centrifugal forces. Tangents shoot out from
the rim; the center is a whirlpool. Why hold
on?
 So here I am, perversely enlightened
by the god of irony, I--a compulsive Leo--
restless, demanding, silent, publicly ar-
rogant...A Dürer Melancolia who knows her
wings are too heavy for flight. Instead:
contemplate Giotto's intense Madonnas (what do
they see?), Botticelli's transparencies, Cima-
bue's fluttering angels flitting about the
dead Christ. Surely they saw something. What?
 I believe in St. Augustine, and in his
beloved, the silent Christ who haunts us
through the revels and gently bends us into
sleep. Silenus in the midst of the orgies.
(Joan would never understand.) "What is the
best thing in life, old man?" "The best thing
is never to have been born. But having been
born, the best thing is to die quickly."
 "Der Tod, das ist die kühle Nacht...."
 It's easy to ham it up, to label the
platitudes--which are simply embarrassed
stammerings in the face of uncertainty. There
are enough puns and witticisms on the way to
Hell. Brutus and Hamlet are blood brothers,
like Cain and Abel. And Macbeth is the Holy
Ghost. The shortest distance is NOT a straight

line but a spiral.

Joan finally came home at noon. "Call me at 8," she said stumbling into the bedroom. It's Saturday. It must have been some party. There must be more to life.

Still, it makes sense in a way. I'm the other side of the moon. Why pick on her? We complement one another. I think if I were doing her part, she would take on my role. As it is, I brood for both of us. She knows it. She's got her own brand of panic. Mine is spiritual claustrophobia, I guess. Shut out forever from light and love. I think one can begin to understand God having gone through that terrible certainty of complete separation. Total abandonment. At least, I'm still waiting for a letter. But HIS--? Never. Never. Never. Never. Never. That too.

Much easier to lock and bolt doors, to cover one's eyes when the Medusa appears. Unless, of course, there is a purposeful self-sacrificing angel watching over us. Or someone waiting on the other side, when panic sets in and we stagger into some kind of insight.

The horror is that we can't choose to be heroes or saints. The condition is forced on us and when we least expect it. And then ...ZOOM! We no longer exist. Something terrible and grand takes over the wheel. One has to let go.

I suppose there are worse hells. This one is enough for me.

AUGUST 30. Why is love so hopelessly perverse, possessive, selfish, unsatisfied, even at its best? We want to follow the meridian to the very top, to the point of light, where all things meet and fuse together into peace. And yet...doubt keeps tugging at us and we stop just short of certainty. Oh we get around it--not making it--find excuses for it. It's always someone else, events beyond our control, something outside us. We even create dissention so as to be able to externalize our own insufficiencies. Push them away. Create distances.

No letter. (But, it's Sunday!)

Still AUGUST 30. I shouldn't have slept this afternoon. The evening looms large, an

unbearable stretch of time. And Joan is
still sleeping.

AUGUST 31. Four letters. Notes, rather.

"Das ewig weibliche zieht uns immer
hinan." The eternally feminine draws us
ever upward. (Dated August 28.)

"Everybody knew of course. Because of
radiation. An inner glow transmits unmistak-
ably. Conclusions are, and will be, leapt to
with alacrity, not without some bestowed good
will, even joy." (Dated August 28.)

"There are more things in heaven and
earth than are dreamt of in your philosophy,
but skinny-dipping is not one of them."
(Dated August 29.)

"The sensitive soul was heard to say:
'There couldn't be too many women who can so
shake the spirit; but I hope I meet them all.'
Of course everyone knew that he was also a
cynic." (Dated August 30.)

How long have I been sitting here? Joan
will be coming in soon. It's almost 6.

I wonder how she will read these?

II

AUGUST 28. If I didn't feel so rotten I could
begin feeling sorry for Francie. Goddam that
bastard in Vancouver! Two weeks out there on
holiday and she's hooked. Ha! So careful all
these months. No casual sex. O.K. So it
wasn't casual. That's even worse.

God, I can hardly stand up! I'd better
get to the doctor myself to find out the
results. Not that I need to hear them. What
else could it be. Cancer? That's too easy.

I can hear Francie already. Well, damn
it, so what? Let him get lost. What are you,
some kind of life-size Barbie doll? For the
convenience of the Georges of the world? But,
maybe I won't tell Francie. Not yet, anyway.

What went wrong, I wonder?

God, it's after eight. I'd better stop
this and get out there. She's got the coffee
perking. I can smell it. Thank God I can
still drink it--

Francie's a good kid. But vulnerable.

102

I mean--NUTS! Months without a man, then...
WOW! And that bastard! For him it's just
another adventure. I could tell. He's a
real smoothie. Probably has a stable of young
eager students following him, admiring him,
ready for him. It wouldn't have been so bad
if they were closer. But who the hell can
commute regularly from San Francisco to Vancouver? Not on their salaries.
      Francie was cut out to be a nun. She's
a girl fit to marry a priest! That was a
joke once; now it's a fact.
      What shall I wear tonight? The big
event, sweetie! Special! Do yourself up BIG!
(No pun intended.)
      George, darling (Donna Reed and Steve
McNally)...I have some beautiful news, tender
news, terrific news, wonderful news, great news,
stupendous news, marvelous news, unbelievable
news, fantastic news, unexpected news (oh,
that, yes!), gorgeous news (like you, Georgie!)
OR....
      Terrible news, unpleasant news, serious
news, stupid news, shattering news, bitchy
news (and so on)....
      What difference does it make HOW I say
it? We all know--every man, woman, and child
--that to George Kilmer it will be HORRIBLE
NEWS! And yet, and yet, not so horrible,
because, Friends Romans Countrymen, George
is NOT WITH IT! He couldn't give a damn.
He'll fall into a role for five minutes and
fall out of it after that. Still, I am the
one who must initiate this exchange. Lights!
Places! Action! Roll it!
      "George I must see you, talk to you."
(No, that's wrong. I'll be right there,
sitting next to him.)
      TAKE TWO!
      "George, you'll get a laugh out of
this--!" (Laugh) No, CUT IT! Just a couple
of seconds, please!
      How silly. For God's sake, he's right!
(But...he hasn't said anything yet!) No, no,
he's right. Oh, I know what he'll say!
      Silly. After all, this is the age of
Aquarius. And the Zodiac is one thing not two.

What about equality and all that? I thought
you were liberated. Man to man. (Something
wrong with THAT!) Oh, hell. It's easy enough
to get INTO these messes. It should be easy
to get OUT of them. Oh, sure--there's
abortion. I intend to take advantage, believe
me. But is THAT the question here? I would
get an abortion in the nineteenth century if
I really wanted it. Nobody would stop me.
Mediocrity always comes in on a good thing,
once it's made legal and "right." The hell
with that. I'm talking about something else.
And if you don't see it, well that's your
problem.

I DID take precautions. I'm not trying
to lure you into an old-fashioned decision.
But, just for the record...what's wrong with
it? Oh, it's not for US, I know that! But
what's wrong with the decision? I mean,
people DO get married, raise families, struggle
through somehow. Is it really so bad?

Look Georgie. I do NOT want to marry
you. I wouldn't marry you if you were the
last gorilla in the jungle. (No, no. Let's
rephrase that.) I don't EXPECT you to marry
me. (Ah, but that implies that he SHOULD
expect to marry YOU. No, don't give him that
advantage. Make him sweat a little. Put him
on his naked integrity. Nothing easy.)

He could say, you see: I never expected
to marry you. Although I don't think he'll
phrase it quite so crudely. He's fearful
when big decisions come his way. He's worse
than a woman. Oh, he'll swagger and boast
about his know-how soon enough, among his
buddies. But...let's make him sweat just a
little....

Take Three.
(Serious now!)
"Do you love me?" (Casually? Emotion-
ally? Buried in his arms? Looking at him
with intention? Fearful? Girlish? Knowingly?
Accusingly?)

Maybe: "Do you like me, George?"
Hell, that's no good. Liking isn't a
strong enough motivation for this little piece
of stage business. YES is non-committal in

this case.

Move away. Don't look at him. No, look
at him, but from a distance. From the bar.
Pour yourself a drink. Ice cubes! Scotch--
a bottle of Scotch here! Half full, only, you
nitwit. Glass! O.K. TAKE THREE. No, FOUR.
TAKE FOUR. (God, I hope it works THIS time!)

"George...." Turn, glass in hand, head
high, defiance in your breasts. "I'll say it
straight out. Something went wrong somewhere. Don't ask me how it happened (hold up
a hand to ward off questions) because I don't
know (take a step toward the balcony and don't
look at him)....All I know is I'm pregnant."

Look out at the Twin Towers. No, turn
quickly and look at HIM. You don't want to
miss THAT, do you?

AUGUST 29. God! I hope Francie doesn't come
in here. I'm in no mood to talk right now.
I've GOT to sleep. George tosses all the
time. I can't stand it.

Why did I stay all night? I should
have told him straight out, early in the evening.
No good. I'm clinging. All the conventions
are showing. Me? Is it possible? Just
nerves, I guess. Did he suspect, I wonder?
He looked funny when I said yes, I'd stay. I
never did before. He'll never believe me now,
that it was accidental. He'll think I'm
trying to get him to feel responsible. I've
GOT to sleep, or I'll look a mess tonight.
Maybe a couple of tranquilizers. I hate them,
but this is an emergency.

AUGUST 30. Nerves! Nerves! I didn't have
to yell at her! After all, two nights in a
row, out with George. She must think I'm
beyond salvation. Whatever that means. She
tried so hard not to say anything--but I read
it all in her eyes. God, that kid annoys me
sometimes. Still...I might as well have gone
off on a honeymoon, as far as she's concerned.
She wasn't always that prissy. Since Vancouver. I'll never understand these things.

Maybe I should just go ahead with it.
Why tell George at all? What can he possibly
do? He doesn't want to get married. I'm not
stupid. Last week he had the effrontery to

flirt with Dee right in front of my eyes.
When they danced, he touched her all over.
The worst part is he wasn't even trying to
hide it. Didn't care one fig. Not that I
care. But it WAS embarrassing. Helen was
looking at me, I saw her. And Sue was
whispering to Ian when I went up to them.
They stopped when they saw me. I wouldn't
have been surprised if they had gone off
together. He's probably calling her right
now. I might as well get used to the idea.
My time is up. So.
  Just do it, kid. Do it. Call the
doctor for the appointment. He gave you all
the details last week. And tomorrow night
you can come home and watch TV with Francie.
Amuse her. Cheer her up. That bastard in
Vancouver isn't going to write to her again.
Or if he does, not for long. I know the type....
I'll tease her and then get mad. Appear
normal. Calm, caustic. My usual bitchy self....
  Still, why give him that satisfaction?
Put him on the spot. Damn, YES!
AUGUST 31. The last supper. Lunch, rather.
Everything according to plan.
  "But I thought--"
  "I did--"
  "I don't understand--"
  "Don't try--"
  "Well--?"
  "Well?" (Out of sheer desperation and
disgust.)
  "You're not making it easy for me--"
(For him??!!)
  "It's not easy for me--" Easy now,
this is the critical moment. Forget that he's
taken your hand. Forget the feel of his
fingers stroking your palm. Let him squirm
a little.
  "What will you do?" That does it. It's
my decision, is it? You don't figure at all?
  "WE, Georgie. WE. It takes two to
tango." He almost pulled away. WHOA!!
  "What do you mean?"
  "I mean, two. One, two. You, me.
Marlon Brando and DEEP THROAT. Shall I draw
a diagram on the tablecloth?"

"Oh, for God's sake Joanie," (pulling away) "let's not suddenly get sentimental and cute. You knew what you were doing--"
"Sweetie, we BOTH knew what we were doing. I suppose I should have gone out and gotten an abortion, not told you anything about it, just gone on. That would have been the KIND thing to do, right?"
(Squirming) "You're upset."
"This is great dialogue. Is that my next cue?"
"You're making it hard--"
"For whom?"
"Oh, damn."
She stood up.
"Where are you going?"
"Where all liberated women go. Back to work."
"But you haven't finished your lunch."
"Is that the very best you can do?"
"Listen--"
"No. You listen. I'm a big girl. So don't push that crummy line on me. The last thing in the world I wanted was this stupid conversation. I read somewhere that character comes out, really, in a crisis. So, there you are, buster. One big zero. Impotent. Nothing to say except platitudes. Cliches. Who the hell needs you?"
"Sit down!" He was getting nervous. She sat down. "I'll pay for it, of course. Is that what you wanted?"
"No, but I'll take it." She was suddenly very calm. Something of it must have found its way into his blood stream.
"Well, what is it you want?" She raised her brows. "Marriage? That's out. You knew it."
"So what else is new?"
"Look, I'm not going to marry you. I told you that months ago."
"Sure. We had fun fun fun. And ripeness is all."
"What?"
"I mean, there's so much else you want to explore, right?"
"That's my business."

107

"Fine." He didn't try to stop her this
time. "So, you know. And you'll get the bill.
How's that?"

She hadn't waited for an answer but
hurried across the crowded restaurant and out
into the street. Why drag it out? It had
gone exactly as she knew it would. According
to the script.

Tomorrow it would all be over. One
and the other. Even if he called her again--
but he wouldn't. He was ready for other things.
This was a very convenient way out. And not
costly. Just a couple of hundred dollars. Oh,
she wasn't going to ANY hospital. She'd make
him pay the limit. Not for the pregnancy. For
being the sonofabitch he was.

One way or another, we get frigged. My
mother was happy. She wasn't liberated. Why
couldn't I have been happy that way? We've
all been brainwashed, that's why. And it's
too late to turn back. I've developed ex-
quisite tastes in lots of things. Sex included.
No looking back. Steel yourself.

O.K. Look at it from his side. Surprise. (Granted.) Self-respect. (He'll pay.
That should do it.) Two consenting adults,
right? He would be able to tell his buddies
without any qualms. (Well, Tony, after all!
It's not my fault is it? I thought all along
she knew what she was doing. And even if it
WAS an accident. Who's fault is that? Sure,
it's been months, but hell. All the more
reason for me to be surprised.) One has to
live with oneself. Justify things. Show your
wounds. Look unhappy. Then, in the privacy
of one's bathroom, you can whistle again and
admire your sideburns in the mirror.

Fink. Fink. Fink. All men. She was
right to leave when she did. Never wait for
the last breath. Anticipate things. That's
one check for you. You read signs well. Free
again. Determined. She'd gone through the
Francie bit. Never again. Waiting for calls.
Messages. Apologies. Dragging things out
until letters started petering out. And then,
the cold shock. It was the same for HER; why
had HE changed? The whole bit. Mooning at

work. At home. Watching soap operas in the
afternoon, for two weeks when she took sick
leave. That kind of nonsense was over. For
her, at any rate. If she ran into him again,
she'd tell him exactly what it was all about.
Experience in bed. Controlled sex. Experi-
mentation, ecstatic afternoons into evening.
You're a stud, Georgie. Just keep up your
vitamin pills. And lots of oysters.

Except for Langmann. He'd already
started hovering. Does word get around that
fast? How does one tell one's boss, she's
had it?

Sorry, Ben. My fiance is taking me
out to Saucelito for dinner. (What fiance?)

Sorry. I'm tied up for the next two
years at least.

Sorry. You're not my type. Besides,
you're married.

Sorry. I'm off men.

No. Better not to start with that one.
He's moody. He'll take me to dinner and then,
when I say no, later, he'll brood. Not that
he can do anything. I'm a junior executive
myself.

I'll ask for a transfer. Newswriting
instead of PR. A good desk job. No temp-
tations.

Ha!

Almost six. Time to go home. To
Francie and her silent cross. Oh well, poor
kid. She'll have to learn the hard way. That
day, when the girls came up to him and in-
vited him to go skinny dipping....I heard him
whisper to Roz. Francis wasn't looking. He's
probably shacked up already with one of them.
Two weeks. You can't expect today's male to
abstain for two weeks or two months or until
our next vacation now, can you?

She'll get a few more letters. Each
time, the same story. Brooding. Waiting.
Sad eyes. Bed early. Then, she'll begin to
sleep a lot. It's only human.

I AM RISEN

Nothing is sacred or permanent. Nothing, my love, is worth a damn. Except possibly admitting it. But that's a dead end too. Who was it said, we're free when we know we're puppets. You almost had me, back then. I really went for that crap. No, fuck you. You WERE right! Why else would I be here, lying helpless in this dark bed, pumped dry again. I never learn, right? So here I am weak and stupid, staring at the ceiling and thinking of the shrink tomorrow. Which one this time? Or is it a different place? Has daddy bailed me out again? Is this home sweet home town? Will Little Miss Muffet make it with the help of Dr. Welby and Dr. Gannon? Time creaks past and leaves me behind. Play it again, Sam! Only this time, for real. I can't stand another cold turkey.

Where's Daisy, I wonder. Probably back in Newark with her big sister. Ha! Big all right. Always big. Man, it's my livelihood she had laughed once, dangling her legs over the couch. It was fun visiting Daisy's pad. Laureen always had a fix for them if they were really desperate. That's Daisy, for you. All the luck. Once, when they were all high, they had eaten the fish in the tank. Laureen had a fit. She loved those fish more than her babies. Sometimes she'd sit, with her legs dangling over the edge of the sofa and watch them for hours. It wasn't often. She was busy most of the time.

You're O.K. for a white creep, she'd say to me smiling with those big teeth of hers. But don't push your luck. Once she really got mad when Daisy kicked one of the neighbor's cats. Laureen was crazy about animals. She'd rather take care of those cats and fish than her own brood. Her big ambition in life was to get enough money to buy a monkey. (No pun!)

So I told her the story one day, about the two old maid sisters and their monkey. For a long time I didn't tell her the story because, well, it's all right if you're Catholic, but Laureen was a Baptist and they don't know anything. I mean, it's a kind

of "in" story--and outsiders won't really
appreciate it. But one night, she was so
depressed--right after we ate the fish--that
I decided to tell her. After that, she
wanted to hear it all the time. Laughed
until she peed. It got so I almost didn't
want to go there any more. She learned
it almost word for word, would you believe
it!
    Tell my friend, she'd say to me. Her
friend was different every time. There
must be hundreds of guys walking around
with that story in their head. It got so, I
could rattle it off, just like that.
    Two sisters lived alone with their pet
monkey. A prize monkey they raised from
birth. ("How did they get it?" "I don't
know.") One morning, the older of the two,
Clara, discovered Zizzie--that was the monkey--
sneaking out the door. It went over the low
wall and disappeared among the eucalyptus
trees. ("What hell kind of tree is THAT?"
"Some kind of tree.") The next morning, she
and Fannie watched. Sure enough the monkey
left the house and disappeared the same way.
The third time, Clara and Fannie (that was
the other sister) followed it. They went
around the wall quickly just in time to see
Zizzie disappear in the church. When they
looked in Zizzie wasn't there. But after
the mass was over, and the church was empty,
Zizzie came out of one of the confessionals
("What?" "A box where you get Jesus again.")
and went straight up to the altar. ("What's
that box?" "You know how people get religion
at those revival meetings? Well, it's the
same thing, only private-like.") Well!
Zizzie went right up to the altar and started
to say Mass. ("What?" "Mass, you kook!
Don't you know anything?" Here I would have
to demonstrate. Those Baptists don't know a
thing about how other people live.) Get it?
Zizzie was saying Mass! He'd watched the
priest at the altar and would come out when
it was all over and say Mass!
    The first few times I told the story,
it was like dropping a case of lead. I had

to explain each time what it was all
about. That's what I mean about "in"
stories--you've got to know what's wrong
with it to appreciate it. Anyway, Laureen
didn't get it at all. But she loved monkeys, and I had to go through the whole
thing for weeks, until she understood the
joke.

Well, it's not really a joke. But
by the time I got through with explaining,
she began to appreciate the fact that the
sisters were very upset. Should they tell
Father Tondo about it? If they did, he
would take away the monkey, or insist that
they destroy it. After all it was sacri-
lege. (Laureen wouldn't hear of that.
She'd interrupt all the time at this point
and find some excuse to leave the room.
Finally--she couldn't help herself--she
told me one day,"You never finish with
it, you bitch. Go on, go on.") So I
finished it.

Do we really come trailing clouds of
glory from Monkeyland or is it the other
way around? I mean, we could be trailing
BACK to something, like in those ads where
the water spills up into the faucet again.
Or maybe we're rolling back time to another
Platonic year in reverse. Zoom! Just as
logical as heaven or hell. No. Logic is
misleading.

Logically, we should all be convinced
of eternity, the mind has no limits, Socrates
and Plato were right. But who can stay up
that high? Here I am, trailing Mind and my
arm hurts. Maybe if I let go, my ears and
eyes and everything else will droop and melt
into a puddle.

Well, that's God. And we keep poking
around in corners to find him. What for?

Everything was figured out a long
long time ago. We're here going through
motions. One way to get kicks. I mean to
try to explain the mess. Like Marx. Although I care for him even less than I do
for Socrates. Why does everybody talk Marx?
He's a dull loudmouth, exhausting himself

on a treadmill. What's all the fuss if
everything is determined anyway? Ah, but
there is always the...final solution. And
then, the classless society will emerge,
pure and lovely. I think I hate that most.
Socrates and Augustine, at least, weren't
fools. They knew what people were all
about and had no illusions. A million years
of exhaustion for a fixed race. A dead end.
    Still, the puppets move. Eyes dry
up. Monkeys are real. The arrow hits the
mark, though logically (who was the Greek
who threw that at us?) it goes half the
distances, then half of that half, and so
on, and never hits anything. Try absorbing
that alone in bed in the middle of the
night. Or try this:
    A cast of five million, each steril-
ized in his own infinite joke. Talk but
nobody hears anything. Panic. Regression
into the length of night. The pitch of
silence. Buried alive in the hum of one's
own ears. Stricken by the desk lamp, now
a plump Martian on six spindly legs. The
typewriter is four rows of eyes and a solid
block of teeth. Now and then it scratches
its flat head and letters ooze out of its
body.
    I haven't been able to use a type-
writer now for months.
    My head is swimming. Have I turned
into a fish?
    I should never have gotten started
on this train of thought. It's frustrating.
I feel trapped....
    I'll go through one of my unwritten
stories. I'll tell it straight this time.
Not like Dr. Welby's tie, a faint memory of
green reminding me of an English country-
side which I've never seen. Is that possible?
    (I wonder how long I've been here?)
    Think Yoga, yoga, yoga. Relax.
Shall I ever sleep, I wonder? Maybe the
story will put me to sleep. It's true, by
the way. Only the names have been changed
to protect the guilty. (I've got to concen-
trate!) Get it right, damn it. Maybe

it'll put me to sleep again....)

Dr. Helen Kramer nodded to the man behind the podium and rose to her feet. The large hall had filled to capacity and was deathly still; a few students were checking over their notes, but most of them were watching the movements of the two people on the platform with the intensity of a theater audience caught in the grip of a fantastic drama.

"Thank you, Mr. Harris." Dr. Kramer waited for the man to sit down, then turning back to the engrossed faces before her, went on in a voice that carried, together with the sympathetic overtones of one who has shared another's pain, the crisp suggestion of efficiency.

"I speak for all of us here, I'm sure, when I say that we are grateful beyond words to Mr. Harris for coming to talk to us today, about his illness. Luckily the experience is part of the past now. Mr. Harris, as you all can see, is well on the way to complete re-habilitation. As potential doctors, you have understood I hope that all symptoms of disease have disappeared as a result of analysis." She glanced at the clock as she ended the sentence, with the practiced casual manner of the experienced teacher. "Next time, you'll have a chance to raise questions." I urge you in the meantime to study the records of this case, which I have provided for you in the library. Today, in the few minutes that remain, I would like to summarize the main points of the case." She lifted the horn-rimmed glasses which hung down her neck on a black ribbon and adjusted them on her elegant nose--it was her very best feature-- to consult a pad on which she had scribbled at least half a dozen times during the hour. Mr. Harris looked straight ahead, his eyes fixed it seemed on the empty seat between little Roy Haleston and Ray Pugliese.

"Mr. Harris' case is not unique," she began again, looking up and automatically removing her glasses, "although for some of us here the reality of the experience may still seem incredible." Her voice was confident, the voice of authority, the teacher explaining and directing. The change in tone was like a signal. Students began to stir in their seats, as though the fascination exerted by the man who now sat quietly in the straight-backed chair behind the podium had been broken.

"I can cite dozens of cases like this one. But I chose Mr. Harris' because his seemed especially suited for our purpose here. I felt it would be easier for you to grasp the subtle relationship between physical and psychological elements in the human person-ality, easier to understand the delicate inter-raction between physical and psychological symptoms of disease, through analysis of a cardiac case than, say, a cancer or arthritic case."

She shifted her weight as she spoke, conscious of the attentive faces before her, timing her words for greater impact. Her manner had the artless simplicity which comes only after years of deliberate and careful phrasing.

"The point is--and this is what I wish to emphasize--once you have accepted the principle that the human mind exerts deep and lasting influence on the human body, physical symptoms can never again be regarded simply as physical." She rested her arm on the podium, leaning forward slightly. "They must be regarded as distur-bances which have their roots in the human psyche, in the human will. Accidents, external events, circumstances cease to have meaning if we accept that premise. The cause of disease and death is within us, not outside." She paused, holding her audience with her fine gray eyes, alive with conviction. "Once the principle is understood, there can be no difficulty understanding the seemingly miraculous cure of paralysis, for instance, or cancer, or asthma, or heart disease." Somewhere a bell sounded, but in the great hall no one moved.

"Said as I have said it, gentlemen... and ladies"--with the barest trace of a smile,

Dr. Kramer turned to the left, acknowledging the presence of the only three women in the class, who sat together in the front row--"said as I have said it, it may seem, I admit, something of an exaggeration. But I suggest that as we strip away the veneers of consciousness the theory I have put forward becomes self-evident. As we expose the raw nerves of human sensitivity, we shall see more and more clearly the reversible truth of the old adage: "mens sana in corpore sano."

She straightened up slowly, taking a deep breath.

"Psychosomatic medicine, I need not remind you, has already shown us the subtle bond between anxiety and hypertension; psychoanalysis has already shown what one can do to alleviate pain and physical symptoms arising from feelings of guilt and frustration; it remains for us to extend our researches into other areas of physical disturbances and bring to light the psychic cause of all physical disease."

Someone in the back coughed nervously. Outside, the impatient sounds of the next class waiting to come into the lecture hall threatened to ruin the effect of the speaker's concluding remarks. Dr. Kramer resumed in her full, throaty voice:

"To do this, ladies and gentlemen, means to gain power over life and death. For psychosomatic medicine is the way to self-awareness and self-awareness is the assurance of health. Disease is simply the outward symptom of a disguised desire for death, a way out, an escape from one kind of pain through another kind, an answer to loneliness. In this sense, alcoholism is clearly a disease. It is the sum total of all the psychic history of an individual. What we are determines what we become, and at a certain moment--at every step of the way, in fact--the physical symptoms correspond to the psychic. Through psychoanalysis, even the most advanced cases are no longer irreversible. Mr. Harris is a good example." She glanced toward the door, which had been opened ever so slightly.

"We all die, of course. Religion tells us it's because of original sin. And whether or not you accept that idea--which is also Greek--the fact remains that death comes ultimately with the collapse of the will. In that sense it is perfectly true that the wages of sin is death. We can conquer disease only when we know what drives us to be what we are. Freedom is insight into necessity, as Spinoza once said. It makes a difference to know that we choose--for reasons not always clear to us --not only the manner of our death but the moment itself."

Someone leaned over to whisper to his neighbor. There was a stirring here and there as the door of the lecture hall was pushed wide and Professor Grant from biochemistry glanced in--an official reminder that those inside were infringing now on the time of the next class. Even Dr. Kramer seemed suddenly impatient to conclude.

"Next time, as I said, I shall try to answer your questions," she finished at last in a brisk, business-like voice. She picked up her pad and stepped to one side. Students began to rise. A few had already started down the side aisles toward the door, when Miss Susan Thorndike, sitting in the third seat of the first row, suddenly leaped up and screamed, pointing to the platform.

Mr. Harris, his arms dangling down the sides of the chair, his head bowed as though in silent meditation, had slumped forward and--as the class watched horror-struck--fell face down at the foot of the podium.

Our father, who art in the ground, make us sprout wings sprout wings. I don't want immortality. Not if it's more of the same. I want...the eternal moment. The all-consuming flash. Atomic illumination. The deafening blast. Transfixed in the completeness of it. That will be quite enough for me. Why drag it out?

Disease is the dragging out of it. There are no perfect hospitals, just

hospitals. No perfect corpses. No perfect
anything so long as one moment replaces
another. But she came close. She believed
it. And for her it worked. For Mr. Harris--?
Still, it's a true story.
   O.K. I've zigzagged to something.
Suppose the will to die is the positive element
in the equation. What then? Back to Plato,
always. Suppose the will to reach back into
oblivion is the final revelation. What happens
to psychosomatic medicine? Are the Kramers
holding back the Harrises, who have seen
something?
   All I see is the ceiling ready to come
down and suffocate me. (Remember the story
by Wilkie Collins?) I can almost hear it
creaking down closer and closer. It's more
than half-way here. I only noticed it after
the lights went out. When my eyes got adjusted
to things again, I could almost hear it
coming down. Slowly, slowly, imperceptibly.
In the morning they will find me, an outline
on the bed, like those figures in the comic
strips that go through walls and all you see
is the outline in the bricks. The Glad Bag
Man. Mr. Clean.
   Cleansed of will. All sins burned to
ash. The bed linen fresh-smelling again and
the ceiling back in its place.
   If I really could choose, I would want
to be a fish kept blupping by uninterrupted
love. Or an eye, acknowledged and respected.
Or a monkey savoring the edge of a mystery.
If Gene had stared at me for hours, watching
me through the glass and the eternal waters,
who knows? But once in a while one does have
to go to the bathroom, and that's when it
happens. Or the filter system breaks down
when no one is around. And the walls and
ceiling and floor and bed and night-table and
me will fuse into one giant transparency--
like a scrim on the stage, where you suddenly
see what's going on beyond. Time will creak
to a stop and transfigure us all.
   Laureen could keep me blupping. She
could keep the ceiling up there for a while
longer. Or Gene. I meant Gene all along.

But then, I've been talking about him all the time, haven't I?

Gene thought...well, even the best of us can't put on a good show. Most of us are Zizzies, dressed up in holiness. No, the ceiling will crash down in slow motion. Maybe, just before the transparency or in that moment I'll see the film rewound, see it as it is. Zoom! Back into the horse's mouth. Laureen and Daisy. The dancer and the dance.

No, I never want to see them again. Most of all, I never want to see myself again. Why was it so easy for Mr. Harris and so hard for me? The will is there all right.

Will they never come?

O golden bird in a gilded cage in Byzantium--lovely in the rigor mortis of art --what do you wish for?

A fix, of course. And in the shattering illusion of well-being, I will make myself immortal. Not an O.D. Not that. Once, at least, I will prove that I'm still free. It will be...something else. Something simple, clean, and deliberate. Tomorrow I will be cooperative (after some initial brooding, or they will suspect something). I will talk with the shrink and scream a little and tell him he's a fink like all the rest. Then they'll send me to the rehabilitation center. I'll go through the motions because I have to get there. It's the only way.

Keep cool, baby. Cool. Cool.

A GRIFFON–HOUSE PUBLICATION

H. PRIM CO., INC.

**38 W. MAIN STREET
BERGENFIELD, N. J. 07621**

DEMCO

William Charles Printing Co.
Lithographers